CLUES TO
THE EXCITEMENT
ABOUT SEVEN-TIME
EDGAR AWARD NOMINEE

ROBERT BARNARD

ALSO BY ROBERT BARNARD

QUANTITY SALES

Most Dell books are available at special quantity discounts when purchased in bulk by corporations, organizations, and special-interest groups. Custom imprinting or excerpting can also be done to fit special needs. For details write: Dell Publishing, 666 Fifth Avenue, New York, NY 10103. Attn.: Special Sales Department.

INDIVIDUAL SALES

Are there any Dell books you want but cannot find in your local stores? If so, you can order them directly from us. You can get any Dell book in print. Simply include the book's title, author, and ISBN number if you have it, along with a check or money order (no cash can be accepted) for the full retail price plus $2.00 to cover shipping and handling. Mail to: Dell Readers Service, P.O. Box 5057, Des Plaines, IL 60017.

AT
DEATH'S
DOOR

ROBERT BARNARD

A DELL BOOK

Published by
Dell Publishing
a division of
Bantam Doubleday Dell Publishing Group, Inc.
666 Fifth Avenue
New York, New York 10103

For information address: Charles Scribner's Sons, a
division of Macmillan Publishing Company, New York,
New York.

The trademark Dell ® is registered in the U.S. Patent
and Trademark Office.

ISBN: 0-440-20448-8

Reprinted by arrangement with Charles Scribner's Sons

Printed in the United States of America
Published simultaneously in Canada

October 1989

10 9 8 7 6 5 4 3 2 1
KRI

AT DEATH'S DOOR

1

Upstairs in the large front bedroom that looked out to the sea the old man's voice droned feebly on, coming and going like waves against the shore.

"To Lydia Thursto, a good and trusted friend, I bequeath . . . I bequeath the silver George the Second teapot on the mantelpiece in the library. To my cousin Nicholas Quantick I leave my Sheraton dining table and chairs. I bequeath my yacht . . . I bequeath my yacht . . ."

The voice faded away into silence. Minutes passed. A quarter of an hour. A dribble of saliva came from the corner of the old man's mouth and coursed down his chin. Eventually, the forehead wrinkled, as if pale shadows of thought were going around in his mind. At last there was some movement under the bedclothes, and slowly a hand emerged from under the sheets—a hand so little fleshed as to resemble a talon. Wavering, it felt its way to the little bedside table and pressed down the switch on the portable tape recorder that always sat there. The voice resumed, with a slight access of strength and determination.

"I bequeath my yacht and all its contents to my good friend Willy Harrison in the firm belief that he will have more fun with it than either of my children. . . . I leave my

Sheraton dining table and chairs to . . . to . . . to my dear sister . . ."

Eventually, the voice faded into silence again. On the bedside table the machine whirred on.

"He's making his will again," said Caroline as she brought in the soup and hot rolls on a tray.

"Good," said Roderick. "At least it shows there's some activity there. I suppose he's disinheriting us again?"

"He doesn't disinherit us. It's just that he barely remembers we exist. It's all those friends from way back, long-lost cousins. . . . I agree; it's the days when he's entirely passive that are difficult to bear."

Roderick, his own face creased by tiredness, looked at her with love.

"The burden falls hardest on you," he said.

"Oh, nonsense. I have Mrs. Spriggs four mornings a week. She does most of the heavy work—and a lot of the nasty work. The royalties from the books at least give us that boon." She thought for a moment. "Which is not to say I won't be glad when he finally goes. For his sake. This half-life that he lives, this twilight existence, is pretty horrible to contemplate after the sort of life he led."

"Absolutely," Roderick agreed. "I shan't even be sorry to leave this house and find something smaller . . . though I know Becky will be upset to leave."

"If we find a pleasant cottage with a manageable garden she can roam about in, she'll soon adapt," said Caroline briskly. She often adopted this tone when talking of her daughter. It served to keep the pain at bay. "Did you write that letter to the *Guardian* about teaching the mentally handicapped?"

"Yes. At great length. I don't know where I get this verbosity from. Father's books were always brilliantly concise. Anyway, I painfully cut it down. I'll give it to Tom if he comes with any afternoon post. Otherwise, I'll take it down to the village myself."

Caroline piled up the soup plates and went to fetch the

cheese. They ate lightly at lunchtime. When Roderick was at school, he sometimes didn't find time for anything at all. A school for handicapped children, however generously staffed, presented a constant stream of problems, and situations demanding decisions. It had aged him, Caroline knew, as he would not have aged if he had stayed at Stowe. On the other hand, he was happy.

"Tom's on his way," Caroline called from the kitchen. "He'll be here in a couple of minutes."

Roderick handed over his letter—Tom was a favorite of Becky's and always very obliging. When he came back into the dining room, he was holding another.

"Who do we know lives in Pelstock, in Essex? Writes an enthusiastic but unformed hand, probably female?"

"One of your father's fans," said Caroline promptly. "Wanting his autograph, or conceivably advice on her love life. Send her the form reply."

"No, it's to me," said Roderick, cutting himself some Camembert. "The ones that don't know always write to him, usually care of the publishers." He slit open the letter. "Good Lord!" From the first line it had his attention, and he read on avidly, his cheese disregarded. "Good Lord!"

"Roderick, you don't know how aggravating it is to have someone reading a letter and saying 'Good Lord!' over and over. At least tell me who it's from."

"What? Oh, yes—it's from Cordelia Mason. My—what is it?—half sister. Dad's by-blow."

"That's an awful expression to use of an illegitimate child," Caroline said reprovingly. "Think how het up you get if someone uses words like 'idiot' for retarded children."

"Dad's final fling," amended Roderick, hardly pausing in his reading.

"Well, come on. What does she want? Why is she getting in contact now?"

"She's writing a book on her mother. She wants to come here."

He handed the letter over. Caroline took it, frowning.

"Can't we just explain the situation? Tell her there's no question of her getting anything out of him?"

"She knows that. She wants to talk to us. To read any of her mother's letters we may have."

"We have letters. I never met Myra, so I wouldn't have anything to tell her."

"I did," said Roderick reflectively. "Oh, yes, I met Myra." As Caroline began reading the letter he said, still musingly: "You can say what you like about Dad's sexual appetites, but Myra was no ingenue, seduced and then heartlessly abandoned."

"I didn't say she was," said Caroline, who was glancing at the last page of the letter. "Why 'Cordelia,' I wonder? The only time we saw Myra she was playing Goneril. Much more her line, I would have thought."

"Still, perhaps she cast Father as Lear, and in some obscure way you can see her point. The patriarchal figure, quixotic and demanding." When Caroline had finished, Roderick asked: "What shall we say?"

Caroline shrugged.

"Well, she says she won't 'trespass on our hospitality,' so there won't be any burden on us. We can take her upstairs and introduce her. He won't know who she is, of course. She can read the letters, we can find a room for her to work in. Becky likes new faces, so she won't be any problem. . . . Unless of course she's one of those intense young people with a grievance about her birth, or something. Illegitimacy was regarded rather differently in . . . *when* was it?"

"About 1960. I was down from Oxford, I remember, and was about to start teaching at Stowe. It was a year or two before I met you. I remember hoping when the publicity broke that you wouldn't be put off me."

"Fat chance," said Caroline, grinning.

"Actually, the sixties weren't *that* bad a time to grow up illegitimate. It was just becoming rather the thing. And I should think in theatrical circles it's never been a very dreadful stigma."

"Anyway, that would make her now about twenty-seven," said Caroline, looking back to the letter. "She writes a very childish hand for twenty-seven. Isn't there something odd about writing a biography of your mother while she's still alive?"

Roderick pursed his lips.

"I don't think so, these days. There would be a market for it. Myra is immensely popular, and a dame, and always in work. Does she actually say it is to be a biography? Maybe it will be one of those gushing jobs, strictly for the fans."

"The letter itself sounds sensible enough. I can't see she wants to do a hatchet job on your father. I wouldn't want her to do that. She says she's going to ring. We can explain the situation to her then."

"Can't be urgent," said Roderick, taking up the letter. "She sent this second-class mail."

In the event, though, she rang shortly after six that evening. Becky was just back from a visit to a friend and was making some noise in the living room. Roderick, hearing who it was, shut the door from the hall and returned to the phone.

"I wondered if you got my letter, Mr. Cotterel? . . ."

Roderick was immediately struck by the charm of the voice. Probably that was only to be expected in the child of his father by an actress. His father, in his early days, had had a beautiful voice and had sometimes read his own short stories on the wireless. Myra's voice was, quite simply, thrilling.

"Yes, I did. We should be delighted to see you. Of course, you understand the position with father—"

"Yes, I do. I've heard about it enough from my mother. So please believe me when I say I wouldn't want to upset him in any way."

"Frankly, he's beyond being upset by anything. We can take you into his room, tell him your name, and he'll smile —but he won't know who you are, and there's no way we could make him understand. It's you who are more likely to be upset."

"Oh, no. He's played no part in my life, except as a writer, of course. That wouldn't be at all distressing to me. What really interests me is whether you have letters and things."

"Yes, we do. Put away in a rather higgledy-piggledy fashion, and certainly not filed or archived in any way, but, yes, we do have quite a few. Eventually I suppose, when he dies, we'll hand them over to a biographer. There have been various academics sniffing around already."

"You do have letters from my mother?"

"Yes. And I think there are quite a few about her. During the affair, and of course *after.*"

"The aftermath. Don't be embarrassed. Naturally I know all about that."

"So you won't be shocked by anything he says—?"

The girl laughed. "No, I won't be shocked. There may even be some photographs, I suppose?"

"Certainly. I think I took some the only time I met them together. Your mother, I remember, was pregnant."

"Great! The three of us together! Mr. Cotterel, I said I wouldn't be a burden to you, and I won't. I believe you have a handicapped child—"

"Yes. A daughter. Becky."

"Well, I'm sure you and your wife have more than enough to do. But I wondered if the Old Rectory has a lawn. It sounds as though it ought to."

"Yes, it does. The church commissioners sold off a lot of land when they put it on the market. There are hideous custom-built houses on it now. But that still left us a goodly stretch of garden, a lot of it lawn. It's very good for Becky to have a bit of open space."

"You see, my boyfriend and I have this tent, and we wondered if we could pitch it on your lawn. It would be very convenient for me, working on the letters and things. And Pat could go off swimming or hiking. It's the way we usually travel, and it would only be for a few days."

"I'm sure that would be all right," said Roderick. "We're rather high up, and there are sometimes strong winds, but if you are experienced campers, that shouldn't faze you. Becky may come and disturb you; new faces always intrigue her."

"No problem. Pat's a teacher. We both love children."

"Becky is actually nearly twenty. Though—"

"I understand."

"When do you plan on coming?"

"Tomorrow, if that's all right by you. With the school holidays just begun, I want to make the best possible use of the time."

"Yes . . . That will be fine. Shall we just expect you when we see you?"

"That's right. With our car it isn't wise to be too specific. Maybe early evening. But tell your wife: *no preparations.* The last thing I want to be is any trouble, and Pat's idea of a perfect holiday is to be well away from any and everybody."

"Well, till then, then."

"Looking forward to meeting you—brother!"

Cordelia laughed gaily and rang off.

Becky was quiet now, sitting with a favorite book of pictures that she flicked endlessly over, occasionally giving little whimpers of pleasure. Roderick sat beside Caroline on the sofa, and they talked quietly.

"She asked whether they could camp on the lawn. I didn't see why not."

"No reason at all. They?"

"There's a boyfriend."

"Inevitably, I suppose, seeing she's Myra's daughter. She probably has a whole string of young men in train."

"Her voice is certainly attractive. Clear, girlish. Not at all like Myra's, though, now I come to think about it. Myra's was very intense, with cello overtones."

"Yes, that's how I remember her stage voice. With more than a touch of the viper, too—though of course she *was* playing Goneril."

"The stage voice and the offstage voice are pretty much the same, I think. She isn't one of those actresses with two distinct personalities. When I met her, she was a very intense young lady, with very little sense of humor."

"The girl didn't sound like that?"

"No, not at all. She called me 'brother' in a way that showed she relished the humor of the situation."

"Well, I'm glad she could see it. If my mother had been abandoned with me as a tiny baby, I don't think that I would see much humor in the situation."

"He didn't abandon her, he simply broke off the affair. That was his right, just as much as it would have been hers had it been she who wanted out. It was Myra who refused all support for the child. And it was Myra who took the story to the newspapers."

"And it was your father who wrote that book. . . . Oh, dear, let's not quarrel about old wrongs. I'm quite willing to admit that Myra was no Tess of the D'Urbervilles. When did Cordelia say she would be coming?"

"Tomorrow, actually. But she said to make absolutely no preparations for her."

"But we *must* give them dinner . . . Damn, the commodore's coming for sherry."

"Darling, she said no preparations. Anyway, the commodore has an eye for a pretty girl."

"The commodore's lady wife will be with him. The only eye she has for a pretty girl is the evil eye. Oh, well, it will all work out all right if we don't fuss. I just hope Isobel doesn't descend on us in the near future for one of her periodic visits. It would be just like her to choose the most inconvenient time. And she's due for a tour of inspection—to see we're not neglecting her precious property. Not to worry; we'll cope. But how would Isobel react to the idea of a new sister?"

Later that night, in bed, Caroline said: "You're thoughtful. What are you thinking about? The prospect of acquiring a sister?"

"No. Though I hope she's more congenial than Isobel. It's been nagging away in my mind that there was something—I don't know—something wrong about that telephone conversation. I just can't pin down what it was."

"I expect it's the sense of—what does Ibsen call it?—the younger generation banging on the door," said Caroline.

"Since we don't have any . . . normal children, we're a bit cut off from young people."

"Myra once played Hilde Wangel," said Roderick. "I should think she was absolutely fearsome, driving poor old Solness up that bloody tower. . . . But no, it wasn't that. I expect when I meet the girl I'll remember what it was."

2

Why, Caroline wondered, do naval officers so often carry about with them a faint whiff of the bogus?

She was sipping sherry and making polite conversation about the roses with Commodore Critchley and his wife, Daisy, and all the time her mind was far away, as it tended to be on social occasions that had more to do with politeness than with pleasure.

It was true. Almost all the naval men she had known (she'd met quite a few through her father) had had it: a phony heartiness, a cultivated lecherousness, or a suspect suggestion of dreamy remoteness that probably came from reading too much Conrad. She rather thought there had been something bogus about Lord Mountbatten, and probably Nelson, too.

"Yes, we have had a vintage year, too," she said, "so I suppose I must have got the hang of pruning at last. The only thing I regret about having so many roses is the thorns. I never can teach Becky to be careful. She finds them so pretty, and it always ends in tears."

The commodore smiled a smile of studied understanding. He was chairman of the board of governors at Roderick's school. There was no particular reason for this: the Critchleys had no handicapped child, nor did the commodore show any particular interest in the children at the school or in ways of helping them and their parents cope with their disabilities. It was just that that sort of job tended to gravitate toward retired middle-class people who had time on their hands and who needed to feel socially useful. Unfortunately, the situation demanded that courtesies be shown and returned. The Cotterels and the Critchleys really didn't have much in common. Caroline particularly disliked being treated as a sexually desirable object—which she felt sure she no longer was, and certainly not to him. The commodore liked bust, and in his lady wife he had gotten it.

"At least the summer seems to be improving now," said Caroline, still on her social autopilot. "It makes such a difference if it's a bit warm. Particularly now that we can't go abroad anymore."

"Ah, yes." The commodore looked at Roderick. "Your father."

"That's right. We feel we can't leave him with anyone else —and the cost of hiring someone full-time for two or three weeks would in any case be enormous."

"Sad. Because the old gentleman lived a lot abroad himself, didn't he?" said Daisy Critchley in her metallic voice.

"Yes, he did. Particularly after the war, when we children were grown up and he had no . . . family ties. He had a flat in Highgate, and he came back there to write. I think he did that because his books were almost always set in England and he needed to be among the physical objects and the places he was describing. But he wrote them very fast, having made masses of notes while he was apparently idling away his time in Italy or wherever. And as soon as he'd finished the book, he'd hand it over to his agent, and then he'd take off again."

"I sometimes think he'd be happier now," said Caroline, "in some Mediterranean village, with some old peasant woman in black to look after him."

"Why don't you investigate the possibility?" asked the commodore.

"Because as soon as I think about it I realize that happiness just doesn't enter into it. Neither happiness nor misery nor any other big emotion. Best let him have his last years of dignity, with faces around him that he's used to."

"The feeling does you credit," said the commodore, heartily and falsely.

They were interrupted by the doorbell. Becky, who had been watching television in the corner with the sound turned down low, jumped up and showed interest. Caroline went over to her.

"This will be our campers," she said, and she and Becky followed her husband into the hall so that they could all meet their new relations away from the hard, bright eyes of the commodore's lady.

There was time for a brief handshake all around in the rather dismal hallway that no sort of lighting could render welcoming. Caroline got no impression more specific than that of a tall boy and a short girl, both a bit travel stained. Then they had to troop back into the sitting room.

"This is Cordelia, Roderick's half sister," said Caroline brightly but casually. "And her boyfriend."

The commodore had sprung up and was doing his very-much-a-lady's-man routine, but Caroline could see the calculation in his eyes. Half sister? They had met Roderick's real sister. They probably knew that his father had been married twice, but Roderick and Isobel were children of his *second* marriage. And this young thing was his *half* sister. Then . . .

Daisy Critchley gave her husband a barely perceptible nudge, and Roderick busied himself getting the visitors drinks. Pat sat down, quite relaxed in a remote sort of way, and asked for a beer. Cordelia said she'd just have a fruit juice. Becky sat down on the sofa beside Cordelia and seemed to be quite happy, as she often was with new arrivals, just to look at her and take her in. More covertly, Caroline was doing the same. This was her first opportunity to look at the newcomer properly.

Her first reaction was one of shock, that Cordelia was not at all good-looking. Second glances made her revise that judgment slightly. She was dumpy, certainly—whereas Myra was tall, or had seemed so onstage. Cordelia's was sort of puppy fat, but retained well beyond the puppy-fat stage. Nevertheless, there was a residual prettiness in the face, plump though it was, and it looked from the faintly bedraggled hair as if Cordelia simply did not care to do much about her looks.

Pat was a beanpole boy, dark haired, with a trim beard and distant hazel eyes. It disturbed Caroline to realize that she was finally disapproving of a relationship in which the woman was the older partner. What an odd survival of popular prejudice! But Pat could hardly be more than twenty-two or three, whereas Cordelia was certainly twenty-seven. Yet, right from this first moment, Caroline sensed in Pat a sort of stillness that made him the more mature of the two.

The commodore was at his most avuncular. He was adept at small talk, and in situations like this he would use it to learn what he wanted to know.

"I don't think we've seen you here at Maudsley before, have we, young lady?" he asked, bending forward.

"No, this is my first visit."

"Then you must see plenty of Sussex while you're here, eh, Roderick? There are some wonderful walks in the neighborhood. Got a car, have you?"

"Yes—we've got an old jalopy."

"Good. Plenty of lovely drives, too. Only problem at this time of year is keeping away from the tourists. Not the best time of year to choose, frankly."

"Pat is a teacher, in a primary school. So really we don't have much choice."

"Ah yes, I see. . . . So this year you decided to visit your brother."

Cordelia flashed him a brilliant smile. It said: I know you are fishing, and I know what you want to find out, and I may decide to tell you, and then again I may not. When she smiled like that, Caroline thought, she was almost a beauty.

"I'm afraid I'm making use of Roderick and Caroline," said Cordelia, speaking tantalizingly slowly in her musical voice. "They have information, papers, that I need. . . . I'm writing a book about my mother."

"About your mother?"

Pat put him out of his misery.

"Cordelia's mother is Myra Mason, the actress."

The commodore's social manner slipped slightly. His mouth fell open. Daisy Critchley, Caroline thought, had guessed already. Now she took over, her hard social manner substituting for his well-lubricated one.

"I think Fergus was away at sea when—when there was all the talk in the papers. You don't mind my mentioning it, do you, my dear?"

"Not at all. Of course not." Caroline noticed, though, that she was fiddling with her handkerchief. Cordelia, in fact, was never still.

"Of course there is a bit of talk in the village, about the past," Daisy Critchley went on. "But Roderick's father is not really a personality to the locals. Not many of them read his kind of books. And almost since he moved here he's been . . . unwell."

"That's right," said Roderick, who had finished getting or refreshing everyone's drinks and now sat down. "It was to be his retirement home—back in England and near us. But his mind started going almost at once, and he simply couldn't cope. We moved in here to look after him. He's never been close to my sister—my other sister."

The commodore, his avuncularity restored, leaned forward and tapped Cordelia on the knee.

"I'll say this, young lady: You're the daughter of a damn fine actress. Saw her"—he looked at Daisy—"when was it? Five, maybe six years ago, at Chichester, in *Private Lives.* Never forgotten it. Or was it *Blithe Spirit*?"

"Oh, that was *Private Lives,*" said Cordelia with enthusiasm. "It must have been eight years ago, actually. She was quite marvelous in that. All sorts of undercurrents, so you realized the play is really a forerunner of *Who's Afraid of Virginia Woolf*? I was at Kent University at the time. I went over with a group from the English Department. We were talking about it all the way home. Not often that happens with Noel Coward."

"We saw her in *Lear*," said Caroline. "It was rather different there. She was fearsome: it was as if she were determined not to allow this appalling monster any shred of humanity."

"Yes. I remember she said that was the only way she could play her. She said the women's parts were all black and white in that play and that was how they had to be done. She certainly couldn't play Cordelia, and in fact she's never done *Lear* again."

The commodore was beginning to get uneasy with the literary talk.

"Well, you've certainly got an interesting task on your hands, my dear," he said. "It's to be a biography, is it?"

"Sort of portrait," said Cordelia.

"And you'll be here for some time, will you?" Almost automatically, he ogled her. Daisy Critchley, almost as automatically, stiffened.

"I'm not sure." Cordelia, still nervously working at her handkerchief, turned with a smile to Roderick and Caroline. "I don't want to be a nuisance. It will depend on how much material there is."

"You must stay as long as you want to or need to," said Roderick.

"I fear you won't get much out of—" The commodore, unusually brutal, jerked his head at the ceiling.

"My father? No, I quite understand the situation."

"Well," said the commodore, patting his wife on the thigh, "time we were making a move. We'll hope to see more of you, young lady, if you're going to be here for a bit."

"Yes, you must both come over," said Daisy without conviction.

Cordelia reacted to the frosty invitation by smiling noncommittally and turning to say something to Becky, who was making noises. To cover any awkwardness, Pat got up, shook hands with the commodore, and made inquiries about swimming in the area. As they moved to the door, Cordelia, perhaps thinking she'd been rude, smiled again, one of her brilliant ones, and Caroline saw Daisy Critchley realize for the first time what a good-looking girl this could be. Caroline and Roderick saw them off and into their car at the front door with the usual courtesies, and when she came back into the sitting room, Caroline said:

"And now they'll be off to the Red Lion to spread the news around the village."

"I thought they said my father was not much of a local personality," said Cordelia, sitting down again. "Why should anyone be interested?"

"Not so much because you're your father's daughter as because you're your mother's," said Caroline. "Actresses are always good for village gossip. And the fact that she's a dame will add snob appeal."

"Oh, yes, the damehood," said Cordelia.

"And the slight whiff of dated scandal will wing the story on its way," put in Roderick. "But you must know what it's like. You live in a village, don't you?"

Cordelia frowned and turned to Pat.

"I don't know. It's different. I grew up there. . . . Mother's lived there so long people sort of take her for granted. . . . Don't they?"

"Pretty much," said Pat after a pause for thought that was habitual to him. "If there's a stranger in the pub, they might boast about her. Mostly they take her in their stride."

"When I moved in with Pat, there was talk," said Cordelia. "But that was basically because he teaches in the village school. 'Can we let our innocent babes—?' You know the kind of thing. They didn't ask, 'What will her mother say?' because really my mother is hardly in a position to say anything."

"Now," said Caroline, "you're eating with us."

"Oh, no, please. I made it clear to your husband—"

"Just for tonight. I've got a big casserole in the oven. We really must have a chance to get to know each other."

"Oh, dear—we didn't want to be any trouble. We've got the Primus, of course, and we were going to have sausages and beans."

"You can have campers' food for the rest of your stay. Tonight you're going to eat properly."

Cordelia giggled.

"We'd probably have had sausages and beans if we'd been at home. I'm a terrible cook, and we're as poor as church mice."

"I noticed the second-class stamp." Roderick, turning to Pat, laughed. "Of course, teachers' starting pay is pretty terrible, isn't it?"

"Abysmal. And I have an overdraft after teachers' college. Everyone does. It's the only way you can afford books."

"And you don't have a job?" Caroline asked Cordelia.

"A bit of journalism. I do any Pelstock story that's going for the local rag, and sometimes I do special features for them. I had a chance of getting into Fleet Street. Being mother's daughter does mean I have some contacts. But by the time the chance came up, I'd moved in with Pat."

"Never mind. Perhaps you'll get an advance on the book."

"I've had one." Cordelia grinned. "We spent it on second-hand furniture for the council house we're in. It's a bit worrying . . . in case the book isn't what they'd hoped for. Still, they tell me publishers never ask for an advance back."

"They don't usually get it, anyhow," said Roderick, who over the years had learned a good deal about publishers. "Well, that's settled. You'll eat with us."

"But we must put the tent up first," said Pat, getting up. "Easier before it gets dark."

Becky thought they were going and began making noises of protest. Cordelia bent over with great kindness and took her by the hands.

"But you can come with us, can't you, Becky? And help us put up our tent?"

"That would be kind—she'd love that," said Caroline. "There's a garden seat at the far end, near the new houses. If you put her on that, she'll be quite happy just watching."

Pat took one hand, Cordelia the other, and then all three

went out to the ancient Volkswagen in the driveway. Caroline, getting the dinner organized in the kitchen, saw Cordelia take her very tenderly down to the seat. Becky gazed entranced as Pat humped the tent down the lawn, then sleeping bags, stove, and supplies. Soon Cordelia and Pat were erecting the tent with a smooth efficiency obviously born of experience.

"She's a very nice girl," said Caroline when Roderick came into the kitchen.

"Woman. Yes, she seems charming."

"I can't see anything of your father in her."

"Nor much of Myra, come to that. Though she is very pretty when she smiles."

"You noticed. She could be very attractive altogether if she slimmed and took a little trouble. Funnily enough, she reminded me of that picture of your grandmother that your father always carried around with him—probably because she was plump, too. They're both awfully good with Becky. The boy seems to have a quiet—I don't know—"

"Strength. It's a cliché, but it seems true. Whereas she—I felt on the phone, and still do—doesn't seem quite to have grown up."

"No. But remember she's had Myra Mason as a mother. Very famous, and I'd guess frightfully dominating. She probably never gave the girl space to mature, to become her own person. Children of famous people often do grow up rather inadequate."

"Thank you," said Roderick. Caroline laughed and kissed him.

"Your father was so seldom around when you were a child he didn't have a chance to restrict you," she said. "Too busy chasing his women."

3

The Old Rectory, Maudsley, was two miles outside Maudsley proper. It had originally served for the pastor to a tiny rustic church and a few agricultural cottages attached to the estate of a landed proprietor, in whose gift the living had been. Then it had been taken over to serve for Maudsley, and then, in the seventies, sold off as being too difficult to heat and maintain. Vicars, these days, were less philoprogenitive than their nineteenth-century counterparts.

The house was rambling, ramshackle, and inconsistent. The good rooms gave out on the lawn, while those on the other side were dark and poky. Only from the upstairs could one get a view of the sea. The new houses at the bottom of the garden were an eyesore, but Caroline had several friends among the women who lived there, for architectural taste has little bearing on character or disposition. On the whole she was happy at the Rectory and did not regret the decision to move in there that had been forced upon them.

The day after the young couple's arrival, while she was washing up, Caroline saw Pat setting off in the direction of the cliff path down to the beach. Ten minutes later Cordelia arrived, bursting with eagerness to get started. She had in her hand a notebook, a little set of colored felt pens, and a packet of sandwiches made with sliced bread.

"I can't wait to get down to work," she said.

Caroline took the hint and took her straight through the dismal hall to a rather inconveniently shaped room off it.

"I thought I'd put you in here," she said. "It was the room your father intended as his study, though I don't think he ever in fact worked here. He liked a smallish room, with no sort of view—nothing to distract him. He certainly would have had that here."

Cordelia looked around. On one wall an enormous bookcase contained all the editions—hardback, paperback, foreign—of Benedict Cotterel's works. The desk was massive, with capacious drawers, and was placed up against a blank wall. The desk calendar was for 1977. Against the wall that had a window in it—a window that looked out only on shrubbery—was a series of cupboards, old and squat.

"Now," said Caroline briskly, for she felt a certain embarrassment at exposing a father's secrets to a long-lost daughter, "you'll soon find there's very little method. I can only say that *mostly* you'll find his collection of letters written *to* him in this cupboard here. Some pretty well known names corresponded with him, and I suppose your mother's letters will be among them. His reviews, interviews with him, and so on, you'll find in these two drawers. But I don't imagine they'll be of much interest. The manuscripts and typescripts for all the books up to 1960 were bought by a university in Texas. Those for the later books are in the cupboard over there. People have started sending back either the originals or photocopies of his own letters, assuming someone, sometime, will do a collected. These we've tended to put in the desk drawers, knowing he'll never use it again. Right? That is only a *rough* guide. In fact, you'll find things in all sorts of places."

"Right . . ." said Cordelia slowly. "I'll spend the morning finding my way around. You said books after 1960 were all here, so that must mean you have *The Vixen*?"

"Yes."

"There are probably things in that that didn't get into the

published text. I know my mother's lawyers were very active before it came out."

"Very probably. I remember that Ben had a whale of a time and behaved quite disgracefully. That was soon after we were married, and I was very prim, and probably too easily shocked. . . . But I must say I've always thought that book beneath him. Naked, unworthy revenge. I read it again a few years ago, and I still felt the same. I don't count that as part of his real fictional output."

"It's certainly unlike the others. Because he hadn't gone in for autobiography before, had he? Or if he had, I didn't recognize it."

"Not direct autobiography like that. One or two of his other . . . women friends claimed to recognize themselves, but they were put in plots that had nothing to do with Ben's own life."

"Anyway, that's the book that's of particular interest to me."

"Of course it is. Well, I'll leave you to it."

Caroline's day was low-key but busy. Becky had a fit of petulance and unreasonableness before lunch, as she sometimes did if she was at home and Roderick was not. Roderick was at a day-long conference of local headmasters. Caroline had a lunch of scrambled egg and fruit with Becky and Mrs. Sprigg, and when they had finished, she asked if Ben was up to receiving a visitor.

"Well, he's a bit drowsy, but it doesn't make all that much difference, does it? Who is it?"

"His daughter, actually. Illegitimate. He's never seen her before. Of course he won't know who she is."

"He won't, and that's a fact," said Mrs. Sprigg. Clearly she was interested and would get a lot more detail out of Caroline before many days were past.

Caroline let her go upstairs to the old man, then went to the study, knocked, and put her head around.

"I wondered if you'd like to come up and say hello to Ben," she said.

Cordelia looked apprehensive, then smiled bravely.

"I'd love to," she said.

"It seemed only right," said Caroline as they went up-stairs. "Isobel, Roderick's sister, never goes to see him when she comes. But she hated him when he was— Well, so in its way that's right, too."

Caroline opened the door of the shady bedroom. Mrs. Sprigg had made him clean and tidy, but already dribble was forming at the corner of his mouth. Cordelia gazed sadly at the sunken eyes, the bare skin and bone of the cheeks. It was more like looking at a skull than at a face.

"Memento mori," she whispered to Caroline.

"This is Cordelia, Father," said Caroline, bringing her forward to the bed, "come to pay you a visit."

"Cordelia . . ." said a faint, distant voice.

"She and her boyfriend are camping in the garden. It's lucky the weather's changed for the better, isn't it?"

There was a long pause, broken only by the ticking of the clock, and then the voice said, ". . . for the better . . ."

Cordelia took his hand very tenderly, then said, not really knowing what to say: "How are you feeling today . . . Father?"

There was no flicker of the eyelids. Merely another long pause.

"Father . . ." said the ancient voice.

"He's tired," said Mrs. Sprigg.

Caroline nodded, smiled at the old man, then led Cordelia from the bedroom.

"I hope that wasn't too upsetting?"

"No. I'm glad to have seen him. Is he always like that?"

"That was a bit below average. He has his good days. Then he usually dictates wills."

"Is that what the tape recorder was doing there?"

"Yes. Sometimes he doesn't remember to turn it on. He never remembers to turn it off. He leaves things he once had to relatives we know nothing about, friends who've been dead for years, people we've never heard of. As I say, those are the good days; at least it means that something is going on in his mind."

"Sad," said Cordelia. "And that's the man whose novel I'm reading." They had come downstairs, and she paused at the door of the study. "Thank you for taking me to see him. I appreciate that."

In the afternoon Becky usually had a sleep. It was a time of respite for Caroline, and as a rule she wrote letters or did anything requiring concentration. When Becky woke, Caroline took her out into the garden and did some energetic weeding. Becky watched, clutching a necklace of beads she was fond of, telling them over as if they were a rosary.

At a little after five Cordelia emerged from the house, rubbing her eyes but looking very happy.

"It's been a fantastic day," she said, coming over, "but I think I've taken in as much as I can for the moment. I'll walk and meet Pat and tell him about it. Evenings are our best times. We talk things over."

Caroline smiled, thinking it rather touching. Cordelia sat on the edge of the lawn beside her.

"I've found the most fascinating things," she said, "and learned an awful lot. You do have *all* my mother's letters to him there—first the loving ones, and then the . . . the others. The last was written when she heard he was writing a book about their affair. It's marvelous—one long screed of vituperation. I can hear her saying it onstage—hear the way she would calculate the lulls and the climaxes, hear where there would be a pregnant pause. Though actually there is hardly any punctuation in it at all, as if full stops and commas would only interrupt the pure flow of vitriol. It was superb. I must take it to Maudsley and get it photocopied."

"I don't think there's any photocopying machine in the village," said Caroline. "Best to put all the things you want copied together, and then Roderick can get it done at his school." She stood up and rubbed her aching back. "Safe that way, and cheaper, too."

"That sounds ideal. I'd like the manuscript of *The Vixen* done, too, and we'd need to be careful with that. One day that will be valuable."

"Valuable? Oh, yes, I suppose an American university will buy it eventually."

"No, what I meant was, when Mother dies, you can put out the book as it originally was. Before the lawyers got on to it. Because it's got some marvelous things in it. There's a scene where he takes her to dinner at Boulestin's and she takes offense at something he says and works herself up to a tremendous scene. In the published version this becomes a quite insignificant little quarrel at the Piccadilly Lyons Corner House. It doesn't make the same impact at all."

"Well," said Caroline briskly, "I don't suppose we'll be around when your mother dies to do anything about it. And, as I say, I'd be quite happy if the book was never reprinted."

"So would Mother." Cordelia giggled. "The thing is, you can tell from the letters that the original version was the true one. There's a letter from my mother justifying herself after that scene in the restaurant. I'll have to have all the letters photocopied, I suppose. You can chart the whole progress of the affair from them. . . . I calculate I was conceived during their third night together."

Caroline was a little shocked, but she shook off the emotion and laughed.

"Not all that many people can be as precise as that."

"Mother was playing Gwendolen in *The Importance of Being Earnest* in Glasgow. She came down to London on the overnight sleeper and spent the Sunday night with him. He'd been up there three weeks before, and then they didn't see each other for a month after that. . . . It's funny: they're always pestering her to play Lady Bracknell now."

"Not really funny," Caroline pointed out. "Twenty-seven years have passed."

"I don't think Myra sees it like that. In fact, she always gets *very* frosty when her agent brings the topic up. But it would rather give point to the line about all women growing to be like their mothers, wouldn't it? In fact, what she *wants* to do again is her Cleopatra."

They walked toward the house, Caroline with Becky by the hand. Cordelia said sadly:

"I suppose Cleopatra really is her role. She knows her strengths. I had a real hang-up about men, you know, till quite recently. So many had come into and gone out of my life—*our* life—while I was growing up. It was Pat cured me of that. . . . Funny, I used to think as a child how fantastic it would be if my father and mother met up again and got married. When I was a teenager, I used to read all his books and dream that would happen. Eventually I thought: But there's no reason why that would last any longer than my mother's other affairs."

"Your father," said Caroline carefully, "was not exactly a faithful man. You shouldn't idolize him."

"I don't. Not any longer. But I bet he was a lot of fun. Anyway, as I say, one thing I want to get is a photocopy of the whole of the original version of *The Vixen*. That way I'll know everything there is to know about my father and my mother, and their affair."

"From *his* point of view," Caroline pointed out. "Has your mother changed her mind about the affair, and about Ben?"

Cordelia laughed.

"Not a bit. She still spits fire when his name comes up."

"Then she's hardly going to want you to print any of this —her letters to Ben or the original book she objected to twenty-five years ago."

"I'm sure she won't want me to."

Something in her tone made Caroline look at her closely.

"Then you'd hardly hurt her by trying to publish them, would you?"

Cordelia's fingers were fumbling nervously with each other, but she looked Caroline straight in the eye.

"You've been very kind to me—to us. I don't want to feel I got here under false pretenses, so I think you ought to know. I loathe my mother. I hate her more than anyone on earth."

4

Of course when Becky had been put to bed—sleeping almost at once, with those noises that were at once ludicrous and pathetic—Caroline and Roderick could talk about nothing else.

"Her actual words were 'I loathe her,' " said Caroline, a worried frown on her face. "And as far as I'm concerned, it's perfectly clear what sort of a book it is she's writing. It's some form of fighting back. That may be understandable, but it makes me very uneasy. For a start it seems to put us in a very false position. Or am I being prim and overpersnickety?"

Roderick shook his head in bewilderment.

"I don't know. . . . I see now what puzzled me on the phone: the coolness with which she talked about her mother. It didn't go with her writing a book about her. But we let her come here in good faith. . . . Of course, looked at in one way, we have no moral obligation toward Myra Mason. There is no conceivable bond that we've violated by showing Cordelia the papers. In fact, any bond there is is with Cordelia: she is my half sister."

"Ye-es," conceded Caroline. "But one you've never seen in your life before now. And I must say I've always felt a lot of sympathy with Myra."

"I know, though I'm not sure the sympathy would survive a meeting with her," said Roderick. "But basically I agree: To have helped a daughter write a devastating biography of her mother is not a pretty position to be in. On the other hand, the question arises: How much will she be able to publish?"

"That's true," said Caroline. "I suppose we would have the right of veto on the letters?"

"I think so. And if Myra could suppress parts of *The Vixen* on grounds of libel back in 1964, presumably she could do the same today. On the other hand, it may be that Cordelia could get away with paraphrase and description."

"If she was cunning, she could still deal some savage blows if the material is as she describes it," said Caroline thoughtfully. "We have to remember she is a writer."

"Very much a dilettantish one," objected Roderick.

"But your father's child. And apparently with her mother's capacity for sustained hatred."

Roderick groaned. He went over to the sideboard and poured them two strong whiskeys. Then they sat in the twilit room, companionably thinking the thing through.

"We can't contact Myra," said Roderick. "And if we did, we know what her answer would be: The child is to see nothing. But it's our decision, when all's said and done: Are we going to continue giving her access to Father's stuff?"

Caroline screwed up her face.

"One feels in a way she has a *right* to know. Children do, these days—like adopted children having the right to find out who their real parents are. People admit it's a natural curiosity to have. That doesn't mean she has a right to *publish*."

"Certainly not. Somehow we have to make that clear to her: It's not just a question of what she can legally publish, it's a question of what *we* would wish to see published. I think I'll have to have a word with her."

"This whole legal business confuses me," said Caroline. "If she gets derogatory opinions of Myra from other people onstage, can she publish them? If she tells about her childhood, about the lovers Myra had then, can she publish that? Granted that the aim is to expose and humiliate her mother —and I can't see any other possible reason for the book— then presumably she will want to drag out all the dirt. The question is, what she can legally say and what she'll be stopped from saying."

"You can be sure the publishers will be down on anything potentially libelous like a ton of bricks. There's nothing more cowardly than publishers. The fuss over *The Vixen* showed that, and that will be as nothing compared to the fuss over this. But that's not really our concern. As I say, I can't see that we have any particular obligation to Myra Mason. I confess, on our one meeting I didn't like her at all. But that doesn't mean I want material we own used to throw mud all over her. . . . I'm very unhappy about all this. We seem, quite innocently, to have got ourselves into a situation which it's impossible to escape from and where it's difficult to see where the honorable course lies."

And so they thrashed around, turning the matter over and over, until bedtime and beyond. It was a moral decision as important as any since Roderick had left the public school where he had taught and taken the headmastership of the little Sussex school for handicapped children. Then his commitment had been clear; now everything was shifting, ambiguous, blurred around the edges. It was inevitable that by the time they drifted into sleep no clear-cut decision had been made. All Roderick did was have a word with Cordelia when she arrived next morning.

"Caroline did make it clear, didn't she, that we'd want the final decision on what you can and cannot publish from Father's material here?"

He smiled as he said it, trying not to sound too headmasterly. Cordelia smiled back, her brilliant, disarming smile.

"Of course. That goes without saying. Don't *worry.*"

Roderick felt a little like a nervous airline passenger being reassured by a hostess. But (like most plane passengers) he did not feel reassured.

And so the days went by, and Cordelia continued to come

up to work, sifting materials, comparing texts, in the dismal study. Little by little Roderick and Caroline began to relax. The heavens had not fallen. They worked in the garden, lay in the sun, and now and again they took Becky out for drives. In the mornings Mrs. Spriggs, to and from the sickroom, made it her business to screw gradually out of Caroline the facts of Cordelia's parentage and the circumstances of her birth, so that anything the village had not learned from the commodore and his lady, they heard from Mrs. Spriggs. Caroline was fatalistic about this. She had no sense that Cordelia would feel hurt or embarrassed by the gossip, and Roderick's father was beyond embarrassment. If there was one thing that was certain, it was that the village would talk.

As it happened, it was with Pat that the matter was mulled over next, and Pat, in his half-fledged way, was franker than Cordelia had been. Roderick met up with him early one evening, about five days after Cordelia had made her revelation. He had walked into the village to fetch a few groceries, and on the way back he saw, turning on to the road from the cliff path, the unmistakable figure of Cordelia's boyfriend: tall, thin, wiry body, with matchstick legs protruding from flapping shorts. He quickened his pace in the sinking sun and caught up with him as they neared the brow of a hill.

"Had a good day?" he asked.

Pat turned and smiled his slow, shy smile.

"Not bad. Very lazy. I walked my feet off yesterday, so today I just swam a little and lay on the sand."

"Pity Cordelia can't be with you more."

"Oh, she will be when she finishes going through that stuff. At the moment she's quite happy."

"Yes, er . . ." Roderick cleared his throat.

"But you're not?" Pat had turned to smile again, this time apologetically. "I can't say I'm surprised. In fact, we realized you wouldn't be. That's why Cordelia took the first opportunity to come clean."

"Could we sit down for a moment?"

They had come to a roadside bench. Pat nodded and said, "Sure." He and Roderick sat, and Roderick tried to formulate his thoughts yet again.

"You see, all we can imagine is that this book is designed to chuck mud at Myra Mason. Destroy the Dame Myra image. If she wants to do that, well, that's Cordelia's business. I can imagine she has a good many scores she wants to settle with her mother. My impression of Myra, on my one brief meeting many years ago, was of a powerful, egotistical person, somewhat hysterical—or at least one that needed a constant succession of scenes. We can see that Cordelia's childhood was probably not an easy one. Still, it's an ugly business, and one we don't particularly want to be associated with. Am I sounding like Pontius Pilate?"

"No, no."

"There's another thing. There's been a battle royal between my father and Myra Mason before. Twenty-odd years ago. Fought in the tabloid press and elsewhere. Most people in the literary and journalistic world have a fair idea of his present condition. It could look as if we're reviving that old war and using his natural daughter to do it. . . . Oh, dear, I'm still sounding like Pontius Pilate, aren't I? What I'm really trying to say is that I find the whole project repulsive."

Pat thought long, in his manner. "Yes, I can understand that. But in fact it's a little more complex than you realize."

"You mean she was exaggerating her feeling about her mother?"

"No, not that. She had a terrible childhood—neglected, abused, even physically maltreated. That's her story, if she wants to tell it to you. I know it's true, because I know Cordelia doesn't lie. But there's another side: She does admire her mother tremendously as an actress. It was something that she clung tight to all through her childhood: She does this to me, but it's part of the process of being a great star. She's seen everything her mother's been in since she was six, and she has a tremendous archive of reviews. She also has a host of backstage memories, and she's interviewed people she's acted with. That part of the book is almost finished. I've read it. It's brilliant. There's an account of Myra's Rebecca West, for example, that's uncanny. It brings it totally to life, so that you feel you've seen it, yet Cordelia was only thirteen when Myra did *Rosmersholm*. That part of the book could be published on its own, and it's pure admiration, almost hero worship."

"I see . . . But in the other part it's to be no holds barred?"

Pat shrugged. "There's no reason for her to pull her punches. Myra is a monster, and Cordelia's been the main victim."

"But isn't she worried the publisher will simply reject it?"

Pat smiled. "Not really. Of course, Cordelia will be willing to negotiate, go into a huddle with the lawyers and so on. But if they find it just too hot to handle, then the part on Myra's stage career can be published, lavishly illustrated. High-class fan stuff. If they put a veto on the other part, Cordelia's going to lodge it with her bank. Her mother will know that as soon as she dies this account of her personal life will be published. That, in a way, will be almost better— a revenge, but a long-drawn-out one, hanging over Myra for the rest of her life. I suppose you think that sounds quite disgusting?"

"Yes, I do rather," said Roderick unhesitatingly. "Revenge is never a pretty thing."

"But sometimes it's necessary. You can't imagine what Cordelia was like when we first met. A nervous, listless wreck, unsure of herself, unable to relate to other people. Myra did that. Deliberately, over the years, Myra did it. Since Cordelia was an adolescent, Myra has made it her great mission to demolish any confidence she might feel in herself and her own abilities. Anything she tried to do was ridiculed, any qualities she has were rubbished. That's why this book is necessary. Cordelia has got to write it and then get on with a life, a career of her own. She's got to write Myra out of her life."

Pat had become most eloquent. Roderick sat thinking.

"I suppose that makes a sort of sense," he said at last with a sigh. "We all have to get our parents out of our systems somehow. My father was a sexual pirate who made occasional visits to the family circle. I'm an obsessively faithful husband, a devoted family man. Caroline's father was a bit of a crook; he had a multitude of business enterprises, and he sailed all of them on to the windy side of the law. Caroline is a slave to duty, endlessly sifting the moral implications of what she does. I suppose some such process is operating with Myra and Cordelia. Not knowing Myra well, I can't precisely puzzle it out, but I take your word for it that she's given Cordelia good cause. You know her, and you've seen the consequences in Cordelia."

"Actually I don't know her," said Pat.

"Don't know her? Then you don't think—?"

"That Cordelia may be exaggerating? No. Everything I've heard in the village, everything I've heard when Cordelia is talking to Myra's fellow actors, bears out what she says. She must be one of the most hated people in the theater, and that's saying something. I may say the reason I haven't met Myra is that she made it clear to Cordelia and anyone else who would listen that she had no intention of bestowing any notice on some scrubby little down-at-heel schoolteacher that her daughter had the bad taste to take up with."

"Did she actually say that to Cordelia?"

"She did. And remember, Cordelia may have grown up a bit twisted—with that upbringing that was inevitable. But she is totally truthful. If she says a thing has happened, it has happened. She knows her mother as no one else does, because she knows what she's *done*. She's had it done to *her*."

Pat had been unusually communicative, even eloquent. Now he lapsed into his characteristic silence. By common consent they got up and began the walk back to the Old Rectory.

Roderick and Caroline agreed it was time to let the topic of the biography be. There was nothing they could do, certainly not for the moment. Soon Cordelia would be finished with the material at the Rectory, and she and Pat would move on. Roderick and Caroline relaxed and enjoyed having the young people around. As they got closer, Roderick seemed to regard Cordelia more as a daughter than as a sister—a daughter for whom he no longer needed to feel any responsibility. One evening they went, all three, down to the tent and sat around on the lawn eating a supper of sausages and beans (they had no positive evidence that Cordelia and Pat ever ate anything else) and drinking red wine. There was lots of laughter. Pat played the mouth organ, which enchanted Becky. Cordelia told some backstage stories, and since she chose them carefully and they reflected no discredit on her mother, they could be enjoyed without embarrassment. Becky was so in love with the fading light, the two young people, and the uproarious cheerfulness that she was allowed to stay up well beyond her normal bedtime. It was nearly ten o'clock when they made for the house, and Caroline went straight up to check on the invalid and to put Becky to bed.

It was while she was upstairs that the phone rang.

"Maudsley 7536," said Roderick.

"Mr. Cotterel? Roderick Cotterel?"

He knew the voice. Surely he knew the voice. But it was the voice of none of their friends.

"Speaking."

"You may not remember me, but we met a long time ago. I'm Myra Mason."

She did not say Dame Myra Mason. The tone of voice said dame. Roderick smiled at the fiction that he might not remember her.

"I remember you very well indeed, of course," he said, making his voice as cordial as possible.

"Happier times," said the rich, velvet voice. It was a voice that changed moods and attitudes very quickly. Now it was in the mood reminiscent. "You were even younger than me, I remember. I expect you were quite shocked at the situation."

"I had ceased being shocked by anything my father did

before I was into my teens," said Roderick. "Though I was embarrassed."

He was at once conscious of having committed a species of disloyalty and of having been led into it. Probably Myra was good at that.

"People tell me that the old man is—I don't quite know how to put it—"

"Senile. Yes, I'm afraid so."

The voice had acquired new undertones, this time of concern and compassion.

"It must be a terrible burden for you—and your wife. Sad, too. Because, whatever else one might say, he had a fine mind. . . . Time to let bygones be bygones, I think."

"Oh, I think the time for recriminations is long gone by," said Roderick. Though personally he doubted if it was for Myra.

"Yes . . . You're probably wondering why I'm ringing you after all this time. The fact is, my daughter and her boyfriend have taken off on a camping holiday, and I heard in the pub here tonight that someone had had a postcard from them, from Sussex. I wondered if by any chance they'd come to see you."

"Yes, they're staying here."

"They're *staying* with you?"

"They're camping in the garden."

"I *thought* she might . . . Silly, silly girl. She's always been so taken up with her father. *So* idiotic."

"Do you think so? It seems perfectly natural to me. Especially when her father was a famous writer."

"It can only end in tears. I've always told her so. And particularly when . . . when he's in the condition he is in."

"My wife tells me she's seen him. I don't think it particularly upset her."

"But what's the point? And how do you think *I* feel, having all that old business raked over again?"

It was the first time a genuine note had intruded into the vocal performance—a note of rich self-pity. Roderick decided to be direct.

"Forgive me, Dame Myra, but I had the impression at the time that both you and my father rather relished the fight."

"Did you? *Did* you? . . . Well, we won't go over that again. I'm glad the silly pair are safe. They're so *young*. . . . One worries. . . . Has Cordelia, I wonder, asked a lot about your father and me? About the affair?"

"Well, yes—"

"She hasn't asked to see papers, has she? Letters?"

The steel in her voice made Roderick feel absolutely miserable, like a peccant schoolboy.

"She has, yes."

"I hope you showed her nothing. What reason did she give?"

"There has been talk of a biography of you—"

"Complete nonsense."

". . . of a *book,* anyway."

"There will be no book. Do I gather that you've shown her things?"

"Well, yes. He is her father, after all."

"What has that got to do with anything? This book is about me. . . ." The tone of voice changed abruptly. "Oh, I realize I haven't been the perfect mother. What stage person has been? We are notoriously bad parents. We can't give them the *stability,* and children are so very conservative. . . .Though really, when I come to think about it, little Miss Cordelia wasn't so badly done by. At least I never sent her away, always had her with me. She had a *home*—a lot of stage children have nothing but a prop basket. . . . When I *think* of the Broadway offers, the Hollywood offers, I've turned down. No, I said, I have a child, and I can't disrupt her home life and her education. Over and over, I had to turn them down. It's the reason my career has never really taken off in the States. And now she does this. . . ."

"Maybe this is just a temporary estrangement," began Roderick.

"Maybe. The silly goose has been made to see reason in the past. Only now she has that long streak of a schoolteacher to egg her on. I think I'm going to have to—"

Myra stopped. For a few seconds Roderick heard breathing, then there was a click. He did not think they had been cut off.

He stood thinking for a moment. What was it Myra thought she was going to have to do? Come down to Maudsley? If so, then the children—as he thought of them—ought to be warned. He realized he had now gone over to their side. He went into the garden, but as he walked toward the tent, he heard the sounds of lovemaking. He turned back and locked the door behind him. There would be time enough in the morning.

5

Roderick went down to tell them early next morning. They were sitting outside their tent, eating eggs and bacon and fried bread cooked on their Primus. So they could manage something other than sausages and beans.

"Your mother rang last night," Roderick said to Cordelia.

"I thought it wouldn't be long," she said equably. She fiddled nervously with the food on her plate, then looked up at him with one of her dazzling smiles. "I suppose news of one of our postcards has got back to her. Did she throw a rage?"

"No-o," admitted Roderick. "Though of course she wasn't pleased."

"Did you tell her I was looking at your father's letters and papers and things?"

"That was what she wasn't pleased about. . . . Before she rang off, she said: 'I think I'm going to have to—' "

"What did she mean by that?"

"I rather thought she meant she was going to have to come down here."

"I think you're right." She put aside her plate and looked up at him again with a sunny smile. "Great . . . just great. Thank you very much for telling me."

So Cordelia didn't seem to be worried. Indeed, she seemed

to look forward to such a visit with relish. Roderick turned
and went back to the house.

Cordelia worked in the little library as usual, but at lunchtime Pat came back, and they ate together on the lawn.
Looking out from the kitchen, Roderick saw that Pat had
brought a newspaper from the village, and they were poring
over it and the AA Book. When Cordelia came back into the
house after lunch, she announced:

"We don't think Myra will come down until Sunday.
She's in *John Gabriel Borkman* at the National every night
until Saturday. Then she has a week off. That's when she'll
choose. And we guess she'll stay at the Red Lion. Though it
could be the Imperial in Cottingham—it's grander, and
Mother likes grandeur. But it's farther away, and we
wouldn't be so get-at-able from there, so we think she'll stay
in Maudsley."

It was almost as if Cordelia were planning the visit.

In fact, that evening, in the Red Lion, where she and Pat
had become quite well known, Cordelia said to the landlord:
"We think my mother may be ringing up to book a room
here before long."

"Don't know about that, miss. We're nigh on full. . . .
Oh, would your mother be this Myra Mason that people
have been going on about?"

"That's right."

"Oh, well, then, we'll surely have a room for her. A very
fine actress, people do say."

A very fine actress, and a dame. In spite of the summer
saturation by tourists, this was a combination rare enough to
startle a landlord out of his habitual cynicism. In fact, he
mentioned the possibility of her coming to his regulars several times in the course of the evening, and when the phone
call did come next morning, he mixed affability and servility
in equal measure and promised the well-bred, throbbing
voice the best room in the inn, though it meant depriving a
good and regular patron and his wife of it. The main use of a
title—as titled people say with such monotonous regularity

—is that it gets you a good table in restaurants. This was the rural equivalent.

The landlord told Cordelia and Pat, when they were in on Thursday night, that Dame Myra was coming on Sunday and had booked initially for three days.

Myra, it seemed, was on everybody's minds. The fact that the father of her child had been one of the great novelists of his generation seemed to have been forgotten—as the old man upstairs, in his senility, had somehow become an irrelevance. Cordelia now, like the rest, seemed totally preoccupied with her mother. On Friday, in some fitful sunshine, she took a break from the dreary study and, walking in the shrubbery, came upon Roderick wielding clippers.

"How did you come to meet my mother?" she asked abruptly, as if continuing a train of thought. Roderick put the clippers down and thought.

"I *think* my father wrote me a letter inviting me down for a few days. He would do that, you know. We'd hear nothing from him for months, and then suddenly there'd be a visit or a letter, as if quite by chance he had remembered that we existed. Only by then the visits had stopped, because they distressed my mother too much and upset us children. . . . He was by any ordinary standards a quite terrible father, you know. Anyway, they'd rented at that time a cottage in Norfolk. That would be—let me see—19—"

"—'60. Probably early 1960, if she was visibly pregnant with me," said Cordelia.

"That's right. I was in my last year at Oxford. He invited me, making it clear he was living with a woman—'a rather remarkable young lady,' I seem to recall he called her in the note. I remember, too, that I was rather flattered that he considered me man enough to accept the situation. That's why I decided to go, I suppose: to show how sophisticated I was about such things. But I remember I said nothing about the visit to my mother."

"Your mother is an enigma in all this," said Cordelia thoughtfully. "I've virtually found no mention of her in the letters. What kind of woman was she?"

"Intelligent, self-effacing, and Catholic. There was no question of a divorce—and since my father never met any-one he wanted to marry and probably realized after the second attempt that marriage was not for him, the question never came up. They just lived separate lives."

"So what kind of establishment did you find when you got to Norfolk?"

"Odd." Roderick scratched his chin thoughtfully. "Or so it seemed to me at the time. I expect I had some stereotype in my head of a dirty old man and a luscious young thing. It wasn't like that at all. For a start, though I could see that Myra was naturally a beautiful girl, she certainly wasn't looking it. Pregnancy did not suit her."

"Probably that's why she's never gone in for it again," said Cordelia, chuckling. "That and the fact that children have to be looked after. Or at any rate, that other people rather expect them to be."

"Yes . . . Anyway, here was this very intense, self-pos-sessed, ambitious girl who'd had to throw up the part of Ellie Dunn at the Haymarket when the pregnancy started showing. I say 'self-possessed'—maybe 'self-obsessed' would be a better term. She was clearly half-resentful of the preg-nancy and wondering what stage offers she would get after the baby was born. She was without doubt pleased, even proud, to have so famous a lover, yet she made no apparent effort to make him happy or comfortable. Her housekeeping was atrocious."

Cordelia laughed delightedly.

"It would be!"

"This was the dawn of the era of convenience foods. They were not as good then as they are now. All the food we ate was frozen, or from tins, and even then it was always over-cooked or undercooked. My father was never a gourmet, but he always liked a minimum of creature comforts. I remem-ber he got a woman in from the village to cook my welcome dinner. The other meals he tried to make a big joke out of, with me."

"It's very typical. I remember at some crisis or other my

mother taking me to a cottage in Lincolnshire, to 'get away from it all.' We had to come back after five days, because I was half-starved."

Roderick was thinking back.

"I said the situation was odd. The difficulty was to find the basis for the relationship. Sex, of course—but it had become much more than casual, so there had to be something else. She was wild to get him to write a play for her. Badgering wouldn't be too strong a word."

"I'm sure," said Cordelia.

"Remember his novel-writing career was over, or so everyone thought. He hadn't published any fiction since 1952. He'd said all he had to say, that was his public line, and in fact his last one had been rather thin. It had been a splendid career, stretching back to 1927, when D. H. Lawrence was still alive—".

"I know," said Cordelia with a touch of impatience. "I did my M.A. thesis on him."

"Really? You've never told us that. I can't imagine your mother approved."

"I told her it was on Elizabeth Bowen. She never knew till the degree had been awarded. You say she was badgering him for a play."

"Right. Well, Father had announced to all and sundry for years that his novel-writing days were over, and I think Myra hoped that the idea of a play would stimulate him creatively. He'd written one play, years before. It had been put on by Binkie Beaumont, but it had been a critical success rather than one with the public."

"Was anything done about a second play?"

"Ideas were tossed back and forth. We'd sit eating our half-heated steak and kidney pudding out of tins, and Father would say: 'What about this?' and Myra would sit, considering the idea in her intense, egotistical way: What part was there for her? How effective would her scenes be? And he would watch her, his eyes sparkling. . . . I have to say it: Your mother has no sense of humor."

"None at all. But what do you mean? Was he just playing with her?"

"I think there was a strong element of that. But there was something else—and I'm not sure that I should mention it, because it reflects no credit on our father: I think he was mostly interested in observing her."

Cordelia laughed joyously.

"For *The Vixen*? Planning it even then?"

"That's what I decided later, when the book came out. Then I realized that that was the basis for the relationship as far as he was concerned. Material for one more book. I found it quite deplorable. Completely cold-blooded."

"Not nice," agreed Cordelia, but unwillingly. She fiddled with some twigs on the bush. "But you don't know how my mother . . . invites it."

"I suppose she may do. It's odd how egotistical people always seem to expect great consideration from others, isn't it? But my father was a beast of prey, a scavenger, just as much as your mother is—at least during this particular episode he was. I'm going in now. I can probably find that photograph I mentioned, if you'd like to see it."

He found it quite easily, stuck in the album that also had the first pictures of him and Caroline together. It was a threesome at the cottage door, taken by the next-door neighbor. Roderick was boyish and sporty, with open-necked white shirt and gray flannels. Myra was heavy and drawn— her face almost bleary, her dress suggesting that she had given up caring for the duration. Benedict Cotterel stood beside her, looking down on her with a glance that suggested some degree of lecherous pride in her pregnancy and perhaps some sardonic pleasure in her depressed and bedraggled state.

"It's wonderful!" said Cordelia. "You must let me borrow it. She looks dreadful!"

As she carried it off to the study, Roderick felt returning his twinges of compunction. It was not pleasant to think of Cordelia gloating over ugly pictures of her mother. What had Myra done to her in the years of her childhood that she should need at the age of twenty-seven to do this? He thought that after a day or two he would ask for the album back.

The matter went out of his head, though, because on Saturday evening there was a phone call from his sister Isobel. Caroline happened to take it, which he was grateful for. He was always glad when it was Caroline who took the calls from Isobel.

Isobel—now Isobel Allick—was a little over a year his junior. His father's brief period of uxoriousness had coincided with a Jamesian phase. Isobel had been named for Isabel Archer, just as he had been named for Roderick Hudson. Neither child, of course, had grown up bearing the slightest resemblance to its fictional namesake.

Isobel had married money and had immediately regretted not having married a man. Her husband was by now a caricature capitalist—gross, blubber lipped, smoking fat cigars at the end of heavy expense-account lunches. He was the sort of figure who might be photographed for a Labour party election poster. Isobel, not unnaturally, was discontented. Her gentle mother, somewhat deterministic as far as her children were concerned and always looking to discern traces of either parent in their characters, had been quite bewildered by her. In Roderick she could see much of herself, but in Isobel she could see nothing of either Benedict Cotterel or herself. Isobel was materialistic, neurotic, and perennially dissatisfied.

She hated her father. So strong an emotion was odd, since the marriage of her parents had virtually broken up when she was about three. Benedict Cotterel had gone off to do something interesting with codes quite early in the war. Thereafter he might visit his family once or twice a year for a weekend. When Isobel was just into her teens, he stopped coming at all. Soon after she had left school, Isobel had written asking if she might come and live with him in his London flat. She had received a coolly affectionate refusal. She had had nothing to do with him ever since. Roderick thought that her real grievance was that she expected some kind of distinction to accrue to her from being a famous writer's daughter, and because of his neglect of his family, little had. Isobel felt desperately the need for some kind of kudos.

"Oh, Isobel, how nice," he heard Caroline say from the hall. Then the responses followed a course predictable from all Isobel's previous phone calls.

"Is he? . . . Don't you? . . . Well, of course businessmen have to keep busy, I suppose. . . . Won't you? . . . Don't you? That's a shame. We were looking forward to seeing you."

Caroline was not struck by lightning for a liar. In the sitting room, Roderick was rubbing his hands. Clearly, Isobel was not intending to pay them a visit. Isobel was quite aware that in the last legal will of their father she stood to inherit the Rectory, while Roderick and Caroline inherited the estate, which included the royalties on the books. She thought this was a most unfair division, but she came down periodically to keep an eye on "her" property and to monitor the meteoric rise of property values in general in the area.

Eventually they got through Isobel's complaints about her husband, his absences, his stinginess, how she "never got out," how their son was proving "a chip off the old block," how she hadn't bought a new dress in years, and a few more standard items from Isobel's list of grievances. Eventually, exhausted, she asked how the Cotterels were.

"Oh, fine," said Caroline. "Busy—what with Father and Becky. And we've actually got young people camping in the garden at the moment. Roderick's half sister—oh, and yours too, of course . . . That's right; Cordelia Mason."

There was a long pause while Isobel digested this and expatiated on it. Roderick could guess the broad outline of her remarks: Little hussy! What's her game? What does she want out of us? Eventually, Caroline was allowed to explain further.

"Actually we get on very well. They're both very nice. . . . Yes, there's a boyfriend. . . . Well, she is twenty-seven, you know, Isobel. . . . She's been digging around in your father's papers. . . . I can't see why not. She's—she's writing a book about her mother. . . . Why shouldn't she have got a damehood? She's a very fine actress. Are all knights chaste? . . . Actually she's expected here tomorrow."

Roderick groaned. He knew Isobel so much better than Caroline did. He'd been willing her not to say that very thing. The direction of the conversation immediately changed, and Caroline's voice took on a tone of strained banter.

"Do you? . . . So you think you might come, after all? . . . Don't tell me you're becoming a tuft hunter, Isobel. . . . Yes, it will be interesting to see her. . . . Oh, I admit we're interested, too, though we've no reason to think she will actually call here. . . . So you will come? . . . You'll stay at the Red Lion as usual? If they've got room, of course. . . . No, she'll be staying there as well, I gather. . . . Then we'll probably see you on Monday. . . . We'll be looking forward to it."

Coming back into the living room, Caroline raised her eyebrows to heaven.

"Well, I really let us in for that, didn't I?"

The next morning, Sunday, Roderick got up and made the tea as usual. He looked in on Becky, who was playing with her beads, and who gave him her smile of delight that her day had begun. The old man was still asleep, but Roderick let in a little light, which would probably mean he would have attained a sort of consciousness by breakfast time. At the front door he picked up the *Observer* from the mat and opened the door to let the cat in.

Walking through the kitchen, he was struck by a thought and went back to the front door to check. He had been right. The jalopy, the old Volkswagen, had gone. He walked around the house to the lawn, but the tent was still there. So at least Cordelia and Pat had not taken off for good. But apparently their response to the arrival of Dame Myra had been to disappear for the day.

6

Roderick and Caroline spent a very ordinary Sunday. They did not see any reason to alter their habits because Myra Mason was arriving in the village. Roderick read the papers and then went out and jobbed around in the garden with Caroline and Becky. Sometimes on fine Sundays they drove to the village while the roast was cooking and had a drink at the Red Lion, sitting outside in the sun with Becky. Today, by mutual but silent agreement, the possibility was not even raised. If Myra had arrived, there would be enough gawpers from the village without their adding to the number. Roderick had a can of beer, sitting on the stone pillar of the wall that enclosed the rose garden.

It was while he was drinking it that the telephone rang.

"Too much telephone these days," he grumbled. "I never did like the instrument."

"You mean you're afraid it's Myra," said Caroline.

"Oh, I've no doubt it's Myra."

It was Myra.

"Oh, Mr. Cotterel—may I call you Roderick, as I once did?—I wonder if you'd be so kind as to trot down the garden to those two children and ask them if they'd have lunch with us at the Red Lion?"

Us, Roderick noted.

"I'm awfully sorry, but they're not here at the moment. The car was gone when I got up this morning."

There was a pregnant silence.

"Oh. How odd. The landlord here tells me that they knew we were coming."

"Yes, I think they knew. But maybe they didn't know *when* you were coming."

"Still . . . Well, if you would tell them when they return that I'd like to see them?"

"Of course. We may be going for a drive this afternoon, but I'll tell them just as soon as I see them."

Myra conceded the drive.

"Naturally I wouldn't want you to put yourselves out. Tell them as soon as you can."

They did go for a little drive that afternoon, perhaps just to demonstrate their independence of Myra Mason. It was nearly four when they got back, but there was still no sign of Cordelia and Pat. Becky moped a little; she had gotten used to having them around.

"*Are* they just keeping away to show they're not at her beck and call?" wondered Roderick to Caroline. "Or do you think they've got something up their sleeves?"

When the telephone rang around seven o'clock, Roderick knew it was Dame Myra. Perhaps, like Lady Bracknell, she had a Wagnerian ring.

"Oh, Roderick—" her use of his Christian name reminded him of a headmaster addressing a trusted prefect— "I know you'd have rung me if that silly pair had returned. Obviously they've gone for the day. We wondered if you and your wife would be so compassionate as to come down and have a drink with us. To alleviate the monotony."

"Oh, dear, I'm sorry you're bored," said Roderick, temporizing and trying to decide whether he wanted to meet her or not. "I should have remembered that you're not a countryside sort of person."

"But, darling, I *love* the country if I've something to do: learning lines, and so on. But *Borkman* looks like running and running—the first time it's been any sort of success in this country, did you know that?—so I won't be able to get down to anything new for months. All I'm doing is reading possible scripts in the most desultory way. We'd just love to meet you both and have a chat . . ."

Roderick hummed and ha-ed into the mouthpiece, really uncertain whether he wanted to meet her.

"It's difficult, you see, with Becky."

"Oh, yes. Your daughter. I did know, but I haven't said anything. You and your wife *have* had more than your fair share of problems, haven't you? Anyway, I'm sure the landlord wouldn't mind—"

"We usually sit outside—"

"No, no. *Much* too breezy," said Myra, dismissing the great outdoors. "I'll speak to the landlord." A minute later she was back. "No problem at all. In any case, he tells me she's over age. Do say you'll come and cheer us up."

Roderick could have said no. He could have said that they did not like taking Becky into pubs because, in the enclosed space, her condition seemed to become the focus for concentrated discussion and sympathy of the wrong sort. He could have said that they had other things to do.

But he had to admit to himself a twinge of curiosity about Myra. Not so much the village's curiosity about a great actress and a grande dame as an interest in seeing how the young woman had developed over the last quarter century. And he rather thought that Caroline—whether she admitted it to herself or not—would like to meet her, too.

"Very well, we'll come," he said.

The Red Lion was an oldish pub, early nineteenth century, much altered and built on to but not yet ruined. Like the Rectory, it rambled, with extra kitchens built on at the back and new lavatories when outside ones became no longer acceptable. There was an element of the bogus about its country-pub interior, but probably no one would really like to go back to the era of sawdust on the floor and spittoons.

Myra had made a free corner for herself in the Saloon Bar. Or rather the locals had made it for her—keeping their distance but taking covert looks, or in some cases unabashed stares, at this handsome migrant bird from the metropolis. Commodore Critchley and Daisy were closest to her, three tables away, but they were much too well bred to stare and were engaged in determinedly genteel conversation.

Myra recognized them at once. But of course, since they had Becky with them, she would be bound to. She rose and stretched out her hands in greeting, and as they approached slowly, threading their way through the tables, they could take her in.

She was not in fact tall: five feet seven at most. But she held her shoulders firmly square, and they were good shoulders. A strong woman, dangerous to cross, that was Caroline's immediate impression—but was it an impression of Myra or of the part Myra had decided to play? She was dressed in a deep scarlet woolen dress, powerfully simple, with a scarf tied nonchalantly around her auburn hair. Stylish, yet simple, she made sure that she was the woman in the room whom the room took its tone from.

As they led Becky over, Myra drew out a chair for her ("Will she be all right there?") and then saw her settled into it with a powerful burst of maternalism that Becky had no need of. Then she turned back to them, the confident woman of the world, and smiled her welcome.

"This is Granville," she said.

The man beside her was tall and fair, and handsome in an actorish way. There was also an air of weakness about him, perhaps in comparison with the concentrated force that was Myra. He gave the impression of being about thirty-five, but that is the sort of age actors and actresses tend to stick at. There was an indefinable sense of his being an appendage— of having the part in the play that would always be cast last, there being so many actors around who could fill it adequately.

"Granville Ashe," he said, shaking hands. "What can I get you to drink?"

"So good of you to come and brighten our evening," said Myra, settling back in her seat as Granville busied himself to and from the bar. "I can't think where those two silly children have gone."

"They always said they'd be exploring the countryside while they were here," said Caroline. "And their little Volksie is very old. It could well have broken down."

"Oh, yes: that's the boy's—what's his name?—Pat's car," said Myra dismissively. The topic of the boy Pat was boring her already. Her eyes shifted effortlessly away toward Roderick, and she directed the full force of her considerable personality on him. Caroline, relaxing without rancor, had the feeling that, in Myra's company, any other woman had to be secondary.

"You know, Roderick, you've grown up exactly as I would have expected you to."

"Have I?" said Roderick coolly. It was a long time since he had been subjected to so frank and unashamed a stare of appraisal. "Grown *old* might be a more accurate description. I rather think I was grown-up when we met."

"You were *being* grown-up, which is rather different." Myra smiled covertly at him, as if they were in some tiny conspiracy from which Caroline was excluded. "Oh, I think the same was true of me, though I had been on the stage since I was seventeen. What could be more absurdly childish than to insist on having a child just because the father was Benedict Cotterel whom I'd admired since I began to read grown-ups' books?"

"Was that why you decided to have it?" asked Roderick. "I did rather wonder at the time. I thought it likely that anyone in the acting profession would know plenty of medical men who would get rid of it if necessary."

"Well, of course we *did.*" Myra was now the woman of the world, old in its way and wrinkles. As indeed most certainly she was. "Abortion wasn't much of a problem, even then, and of course, though it cost a fortune, your father would have paid. No, I wanted to have Benedict Cotterel's child. It was as simple as that. I'd adored his novels for years: *The Great Conspiracy; A Far View of Beaconsleigh;* all of them. . . . They'd all been published years before, decades before, but they were totally real and contemporary to me. I wanted to have his child." She shrugged her shoulders abruptly, as if to shake off her folly or chase off a mood. "How is he?"

"Much as ever," said Roderick.

"You can leave him?"

"Oh, yes. Not too long, but we can leave him. He's asleep now, and he'll sleep until morning. In the daylight hours he has some sort of fitful mental life."

"Oh, is he still in possession of several of his faculties?" said Myra, unable to keep the spite out of her voice. "I'd understood he was a complete vegetable."

Roderick left a second's pause to register disapproval. If Myra noticed, she did not change her expression. Then he said simply: "No, he's not a complete vegetable."

Caroline, left out in the conversation cold, was taking the opportunity to assess Myra. A dominant woman, and one of chameleon moods—or was it chameleon *acts*? An actress who would not take direction easily, unless it was very intelligent direction that acknowledged her central position in the play. There was another still stronger sense she had, and that was of a *unwise* woman—if not in her profession, then in her private, life. The sort of woman who might snatch disaster from the jaws of triumph. But perhaps she had this sense not from the woman herself but from what Cordelia had told her.

Myra had switched mood again, back to one of reminiscence.

"He was a wonderful lover, you know."

"Was he?" Roderick asked cautiously. "My impression was that he was rather inconsiderate."

"Myra means sex," said Granville Ashe.

"Yes, I meant sex," agreed Myra, glancing at him slyly to see if she was embarrassing him. Roderick shrugged.

"That is something his son would know nothing about."

"Did your mother never talk about it?"

"*No.* My mother certainly didn't talk about it."

"Funny . . . Aren't people funny? . . . Anyway, that's

why I had it. Had her. Cordelia. And I've spent all my time since trying to find out what to do with her."

"She seems to me," said Caroline, "a very nice girl."

It was a banality, dropped into the conversation from the sidelines, but it caught Myra on the raw.

"Does she? Does she? Then why is she doing this to *me*?"

Myra, having ignored her for the last ten minutes, turned on Caroline the smoldering force of her personality. Caroline had the impression that this was the first time in the conversation that she was not acting.

"Keep calm, Myra," said Granville Ashe. "This will all work itself out if we can just talk it over coolly."

Myra ignored him. She turned back to Roderick.

"You are clear, aren't you, what she intends to do to me? She is writing that book to crucify me."

Roderick decided that Ashe was sensible in trying to play it cool. Whether Myra would ever accept any other way but high drama was another matter.

"I don't think that's entirely the case," he said carefully. "I know Cordelia admires you intensely as an actress. A great part of the book—the intended book—will be taken up with your stage career."

"And the rest will be mudslinging. Which part of the book do you think the tabloids will be interested in? My brilliant performance in Strindberg?"

"No, of course not. Is that what you are mainly worried about? The popular press?"

Myra scowled, her first ugly expression of the evening.

"It doesn't make me happy. We have the worst press in the world, and the thing they hate most is anyone with any sort of intellectual pretensions or anyone with any sort of talent at all. They revel in the sort of thing Cordelia is planning to serve up to them. Remember Joan Crawford's daughter, Bette Davis's daughter—the press had a field day."

"You used—" Roderick began, and then stopped.

"You were going to say," said Myra unpleasantly, "that I

used the popular press against your father. Quite right. I did. I had no other weapon."

The idea that Cordelia was not too lavishly endowed with weapons, either, was too obvious to need expression. Certainly nobody dared express it.

"In any case," said Roderick, "it's fairly clear that you can stop the book if you want to. The libel laws are not so very different now from what they were in 1964."

"You forget: I didn't stop *The V*— your father's horrible book. I merely managed to get certain passages changed or omitted. The book came out, and it did me immense damage. It was to preempt the damage it would do that I took the whole story to the gutter press."

That seemed to Caroline like taking a can of petrol to a raging fire. Once again she didn't say so. Conversation with Myra seemed predicated on not saying some very obvious things.

"Well, well," said Roderick, "I don't know that it really helps to rake over old coals. Though that's what the popular papers will do if they get wind of Cordelia's book. I must confess I like the idea of it more than you do. For Father's sake and for ours. And I don't think it will do Cordelia as much good as she thinks to get things out into the open."

Myra had begun to smile and lean forward during this speech, scenting an ally. At the last words she drew back.

"What things?"

Roderick immediately regretted his words.

"I don't know. They've confided nothing to me, I assure you. Tales of her upbringing? Your . . . husbands, and so on?"

Myra made an impatient gesture, brushing off her husbands as if they were nothing. As perhaps they were.

"I can't see why she should hold them against me. Most of them were perfectly kind to her. Except Louis, of course. Louis was a sadist, in every possible sense of the word. But I was only married to Louis about a year. I soon showed him I wasn't the victim kind."

There was silence around the table. Then Caroline decided this time to say the obvious.

"A year can be a long time to a child."

Myra ignored her.

"No. It's me she's getting at. Something I did. . . ." A reminiscent expression suggested she was surveying a whole range of incidents to discover which it could be. But after a moment the warm social manner, a Candida sort of role, was assumed again. "Oh, dear, it's so easy to *do* things and then find other people have taken them entirely *wrongly,* isn't it?" She smiled at Roderick and did that little shrugging gesture that preceded a change of subject. "No doubt I'll soon find out. As you say, maybe we can come to some sort of a *modus vivendi.* Tell me about yourselves. And about poor old Ben. How long has he been . . . in his present state?"

It seemed to Roderick that they were shifting from one prickly subject to another.

"Oh, quite a while. Ten years or more, though not so bad at first, of course. It came on quite suddenly."

"Suddenly? I thought these things were usually gradual?"

"Perhaps I used the wrong word. Maybe it was our noticing it that was sudden. We were all on holiday in the south of France, at my father-in-law's villa. Ben had just finished one of his travel books, the one on the Dolomites."

"Godly Heights?"

"You've read it?"

"Oh, yes. The fact that I detested him didn't stop me reading his books."

You read it to see if there were any references to yourself, thought Caroline.

"Anyway, when he came to us, we noticed that he wasn't functioning as he always had done: wasn't taking in what we said, couldn't remember what he'd done the day before, would make decisions and then wander round distressed because he couldn't remember what they were. He was half-conscious of what was happening, which made it worse. Sometimes we found him crying. We brought him back to

England, hoping the more familiar scene would jog him back to his usual alertness."

"And it didn't?" Myra's voice surely had an undertone of satisfaction.

"No," Roderick said simply. "We found that he couldn't cope. He wouldn't go out, or down to the village, in case he made a fool of himself. He couldn't understand his business affairs—and he had always prided himself on that. I remember I had to read the proofs of *Godly Heights*. Quite soon we had to move in and take over the care of him."

"Such a burden. In addition to everything else." Myra addressed the remark to Roderick, though it might more justly have been directed to Caroline.

"Does he need much nursing?" Granville Ashe asked Caroline, perhaps to cover Myra's rudeness, perhaps to assert that they both existed.

"Oh, I have help. The royalties from the books provide that. And he is very passive—never troublesome or aggressive, as one might have expected."

"Would one have expected that?" Myra asked the ceiling. "Ben was always essentially an observer. A silken, soft-spoken observer. . . . It's terrible to think of him with nothing to observe. . . . You know, I've often regretted the fuss over *The Vixen*. In an odd way it poisoned the relationship with Cordelia."

Roderick did not believe that. The relationship with Cordelia had been poisoned by things that Myra had done to Cordelia. Now Myra was reinventing the past to cast herself in the role of helpless victim. He wondered whether she had ever once considered the relationship in terms of the child's needs, expectations, hopes. Yet for all her selfishness and self-dramatization, Roderick could not help seeing something pitiful in Myra. There is always something pathetic about egotists, for life can never give them all the things they expect for themselves.

"Becky is getting restive," whispered Caroline.

Myra, in her rapid changes of mood and pose, had presented a fascinating spectacle for Becky for a time. But

Myra had taken no notice of her since the first moments. Becky needed some reciprocation, some sympathetic response. Now she was becoming bored, making the little noises that she sometimes made when she was working up to a tantrum.

"Oh, dear, must you go?" asked Myra with no great regret in her voice. "It's been so interesting, talking over old times, renewing old friendships." There was never any friendship, thought Roderick. Myra looked at her watch. "Well, even if the children are back, there's not much point in sending them down here now. Far better not to enter into delicate matters when one is tired, don't you agree? Best they come to lunch or dinner tomorrow. Tell Cordelia to phone me. We can have a pleasant meal *à quatre*. Talking about any and everything except that damned book. Then Cordelia and I can get down to the nitty-gritty. Though perhaps, Granville, you ought to be present. You do provide a stabilizing influence."

Granville looked apprehensive.

"No, *thanks.*"

"Darling, it's worth a try. And in a sense you are a sort of outsider. Remember, Cordelia has hardly met you, and certainly not since you became my husband."

Roderick paused in the business of collecting things together.

"Oh—I'm awfully sorry, Myra. I didn't realize you two were married."

"It was in the *Times.*"

"I'm afraid I skip over the social pages rather rapidly. Many congratulations, anyway."

Myra smiled graciously, Granville Ashe awkwardly.

"Yes," said Myra, "we've been married almost three weeks. It's good to have a husband again, to look after my interests."

But few people could doubt that Myra Mason could look after her own. As she saw them to the door, the very tables seemed to shift out of her way, acknowledging the concentrated force of her personality.

7

It was very late when Pat and Cordelia arrived back at the
Rectory. Roderick saw them in the driveway, getting out of
their ancient Volkswagen, as he went up to bed. Cordelia
had a large canvas bag with her and was looking very
pleased with herself. Pat looked less happy.

Roderick went down the lawn to give them Myra's message as they sat eating breakfast (ham and large chunks of
bread). Cordelia said: "Thanks."

"You will ring her, won't you?"

She shrugged. "I suppose so. Yes, I'll ring her sometime
during the day."

Roderick lingered awkwardly. "We didn't realize your
mother had married again."

Cordelia was unfazed. "Oh, has she? Who is it?"

"A man called Granville Ashe."

"Hmm. I *think* I've met him. Can't quite remember. It's a
bad sign when she marries again. The marriages always
break up quicker than the affairs."

"He seemed a pleasant enough chap. I think he is hoping
to act as peacemaker."

Cordelia smiled secretively. "He is unlikely to be success-
ful."

Roderick was forced to leave it at that.

The Cotterels' day was dominated by the arrival of Isobel. As soon as she reached the Red Lion in Maudsley, she phoned for Roderick to come and fetch her. Caroline greeted her on the front porch half an hour later. She was wearing a Zandra Rhodes outfit that Caroline thought would have looked well on a younger woman. It was flouncy, garish, and it contrasted oddly with Isobel's air of perennial discontent. It also, incidentally, gave the lie to her moans about never being allowed to buy new clothes. This was from this spring's collection.

Isobel's behavior when she arrived at the Rectory was pretty much unvarying. She marched into the sitting room, cast a proprietary glance around it, sat herself on the sofa, made another more leisurely proprietary survey, then took out her cigarette holder and lit a cigarette. All these actions annoyed Caroline intensely. She couldn't make up her mind whether Isobel realized this or not. Certainly it would not have worried her if she had. Watching her swing one leg over another in an attempt at easy elegance, Caroline took refuge in satire: She thinks she's in a Noel Coward play, she thought, but she wouldn't even make it into a Terence Rattigan.

"This room looks all right," said Isobel, rather as if she were a building inspector. "But then, it always looks better in summer. Basically it's rather a dreary house. I can't think why Father bought it. I pity you, having to live here. If I do split up from Cyril when Father dies, I shan't live here."

That, at any rate, was a relief.

"Father's very vague today," said Roderick.

Isobel shrugged. "I'm surprised you notice the difference day by day. *Don't* ask me if I want to go up and see him."

"I wasn't going to."

"Old monster . . . Why should I show any concern for him? He never showed any for us. Especially for *me* . . . Now, tell me about Dame Myra. She's there, I gather, at the Red Lion, but I haven't seen her yet. I heard a whisper that you were summoned to the Presence last night."

"That's right," said Roderick carefully. Why was one always careful with Isobel? Somehow there was a sort of neurotic intensity about her that made her untrustworthy. "We had a drink with her and her husband."

"*Hus*band?"

"A very new one, we gathered."

"Really! And what was *she* like?"

"Perfectly friendly, for the most part. . . . Changeable, unpredictable, rather grand . . ."

Roderick was conscious of a door opening, and Cordelia's head poked into the room.

"You're talking about my mother. You have no idea how grand she can be. You should have seen her at the investiture, upstaging her sovereign."

"Cordelia—this is my sister Isobel."

He deliberately hadn't said "your sister Isobel." Isobel had risen and was looking at her appraisingly in a way that verged on the rude.

"Oh, you're the . . ."

"That's right. I'm the . . ." Cordelia gave a quick, nervous smile and turned back to Roderick. "I just thought I'd tell you that I've rung Mother. Pat and I are to go and have dinner with her tonight. So she won't be troubling you again."

She smiled and withdrew quickly.

"Well, *she's* no beauty," said Isobel, making no attempt to moderate her voice.

"That's what I thought at first," said Caroline in a conversational tone, ignoring the spite. "But she has a wonderful smile, and you realize all the elements of a lovely face are there."

"Hmmm," said Isobel, sitting down. "Now—tell me more about Myra."

And so they mulled over Myra Mason and her husband. Or rather, Isobel shot questions at them, and they answered them carefully and distantly. Why this should be so was pondered over by Caroline as much as by Roderick. Certainly they felt no sort of loyalty to Myra. But Isobel was so patently pathetic, inadequate, and spiteful that there could only have been a mean pleasure in mulling over the short-comings of someone who, in spite of everything, was in her acting tinged with greatness. Again, neither she nor Roderick was a gossip, but she could make the distinction between gossip that sprang from gusto and gossip that sprang from spite. Isobel's was certainly the latter. But for all their reserve, she hammered on until she was satisfied she had got out of them everything they intended telling her. Then she announced she was going.

"Oh, aren't you staying for lunch?" asked Caroline.

"Not this time." She invariably had on past visits, raising her eyebrows over imagined inadequacies in Caroline's cooking or presentation. "I'll get back to the Red Lion, to see what's going on. You'll drive me, Roderick?"

"Of course."

"Will you be coming to the Red Lion for a drink to-night?"

"I think not. Best to leave Cordelia and her mother to sort out things between them, without us around."

"Perhaps you're right," said Isobel, who didn't seem at all disappointed. Doubtless she wished to observe all she could, undistracted.

When Isobel arrived back at the Red Lion, she was cast down to find that Myra was not in the bar. The pub was packed, but she was absent. By dint of throwaway questions (which the landlord laughed up his sleeve about), she established that Dame Myra and her husband, after taking a call from her daughter, had gone out for a drive, taking a packed lunch with them. They were not expected back before dinner. Isobel became petulant. She teetered on the verge of petulance for most of her waking hours. She drank a couple of gin and tonics, ate a portion of pub lasagna, surveying disgruntledly the customers of the Saloon Bar—locals, motorists, walkers dropping in, hotel guests. Then she went upstairs and treated herself to a long lie-down.

When she awoke, it was early evening. She bathed luxuriously long, brooded over the clothes she had brought with her, and finally selected another incongruously bright and

youthful dress. Then she spent much time with pots and
bottles in front of her dressing-table mirror. That she
looked, at the end of the session, like an embalmed galah she
was quite unaware.

When she opened the door to her bedroom, which was
close to the top of the stairs, she heard noises from the bars.
She nodded, satisfied. She went down the stairs in a parody
of aristocratic poise and stood at the door to the Saloon Bar.
Again, it was very crowded. A few locals, but mostly hotel
guests having a drink before dinner. However, this time, at
the far end, unmistakably making herself the center of the
room, she spotted Myra Mason. Beside her was what Isobel
decided was a very nice looking young man. (Isobel, doubtless in reaction to her husband, went for fair and willowy
men with a facile middle-class charm.) With their backs to
her were two young people. Father's bastard and her lover,
Isobel said to herself. She got herself a medium sherry from
the bar, then made for a table with an empty chair, not too
far from the Myra Mason group.

"Is this free?"

The woman on the other side of the table smiled, nodded,
and went back to her book. Isobel thought vaguely that
she'd seen her before. The Red Lion had a large number of
summer regulars; probably she'd been staying there on one
of her previous visits. Isobel glanced covertly at the book.
The Radiant Way. Not one of her father's. Isobel was always
hoping that her father's novels would go out of fashion.
That would serve Roderick and Caroline right! Then she
would be found to have done better out of the will.

She settled down, not displeased that the other woman
was disinclined to talk. She slipped a cigarette into her little
gold holder and lit up. She leaned back, relaxed, into her
chair, apparently looking through the window at the
Downs, stretching green and lush into the distance, but in
fact noting and remembering everything that happened at
Dame Myra's table. The atmosphere there was apparently
quite genial. That was a disappointment. Isobel was banking
on a tremendous scene, the details of which she would retail

to her hairdresser, her manicurist, and the few friends she had. Well, there was still time for one.

As the Myra Mason party prepared to go in to dinner and were gathering together their things (though most of the "things" were Myra's), they were stalled by one of those intrusions that Isobel imagined were frequent with the rich and famous. Someone she vaguely knew (a *naval* man—that's right; she'd met him last year in this very pub, a friend of Roderick's, or on the school governing board, or something of that sort) went over and scraped an introduction through the little bastard. He succeeded in delivering what were obviously a few standard compliments on Myra's stage performances, shook her hand, and introduced his busty and bossy-looking wife. Then—Myra having left a pregnant pause in the conversation—the pair retreated, and the Mason party made its way toward the dining room, Myra smiling graciously at the drinkers standing in her path.

Isobel left it five minutes. She had always intended to scrape a few words with Dame Myra, and the intrusion of the naval person whose name she could not remember had made up her mind. She had a damned sight better reason for making herself known than he had, she told herself. She downed her drink, smiled at the Drabble reader, and said: "I really feel like my dinner," as if she had just come back from a stiff hike over the Downs. Then she went toward the dining room.

She was known to the waitresses. She indicated a table by the window with a distant view of the sea and left her handbag on it. But instead of sitting down, she sailed over to the table on the other side of the room where Myra Mason and her party were beginning their soup.

"I couldn't resist having a few words," she said, in her high, sharp voice, addressing herself mainly to Dame Myra as the obvious Queen Bee of the table. "I'm Cordelia's—stepsister, is it? Rather an unusual relationship, anyway. And I thought that now Cordelia had made contact with Roderick and Caroline, we ought at least to make ourselves known to each other. I live in Wiltshire—a large house, modern but large—and *any* time Cordelia would care to come and pay us a visit"—she turned to her, now breathlessly ingratiating—"you and your, er, friend, my dear, of course—please just ring and we'd be over the moon. I'm just itching to get better acquainted, and I know my husband and son will feel the same. Well, I won't interrupt your meal. I'm sure you've got lots of family gossip to catch up on. But do you mind if I just say, Dame Myra, how much I've enjoyed your stage and television work? It sounds silly, but I've always felt quite *proud,* seeing you, because of the connection. I just loved you in *Separate Tables.* That, to me, is what acting is all about. Well, I won't keep you. . . ."

And she smiled a bright, brittle smile and retreated to her table.

"Ben always said that one of his children was a prig and the other was a fool," said Myra in a voice that, if not intended to carry, was certainly not designed to keep private.

"And you've never done *Separate Tables,*" said Cordelia.

"She's probably mixing it up with *Antony and Cleopatra,*" said Myra. "Though it could have been a deliberate insult. With a fool you can never tell."

"I think my father was unfair to call Roderick a prig," said Cordelia, pushing her soup bowl away. "I don't find him so at all."

"Don't you?" asked Myra. "All that business of devoting himself to teaching backward children—little pudding bowls who can't wipe their noses properly? Such nonsense to leave a good school like Stowe to do that. As if he felt *guilty* about having an idiot child himself. Oh, no—he's a prig; a highly articulate and intelligent one. But most prigs are like that."

She delivered her judgments as if no other opinion was possible. The soup was succeeded by game pie. The menu at the Red Lion was restricted: one meat and one fish dish as the main course. It was traditional British cooking, but good and imaginative and ideal for those who had gone in for vigorous physical pursuits during the day. Myra ate what was put before her as if quite indifferent to food, which indeed she was.

"I didn't mean to imply that all teachers were prigs," she said offhandedly to Pat. "But why do you stay in the job when the pay is abysmal?"

Pat found it difficult to light on a reply that did not sound priggish.

"Jobs are not two-a-penny these days. So far I've found I enjoy teaching."

"But you're not intending to be stuck in a village primary school for the rest of your life?"

Cordelia turned to Granville Ashe with a sweet smile. "Are you intending to be stuck in provincial rep for the rest of your life?"

It was a sticky moment. Myra looked daggers, but Ashe decided to laugh it off. *"Touché,"* he said.

"The situation is not comparable at all," said Myra sharply. "I am merely trying to establish, in as tactful a manner as possible, what kind of support my daughter will have if, as you say, this . . . union—affair, whatever you want to call it—is intended to be permanent."

"Quite a lot of the teachers at the Pelstock Primary School are married," said Pat mildly. "I haven't noticed that any of them are starving."

"You missed out the bit about 'the manner to which she is accustomed,' Mother," said Cordelia. "The heavy-father act is ridiculous in this day and age, and the heavy-mother act still more so. Anyway, the manner to which I was accustomed was always a pretty rackety manner."

"Rackety! When I think what I shielded you from!"

"What I remember is the stuff that got past the shield. Why don't you just accept the fact that Pat and I are living together and intend to go on doing so? Is it harming you? Surely it makes you freer. What should you have said to your parents if they tried to put a stop to your affair with Benedict Cotterel?"

"What I *would* have said I don't know, but what I *should* have said is 'Thank you very much,'" said Myra Mason through clenched teeth.

"This discussion is getting out of hand," said Granville

Ashe. "And it's quite unnecessary. Myra has accepted that you two are living together. She's just worried that you won't have enough to live on."

"Well, don't be," said Cordelia. Myra stared gloomily at her plate. "How's *John Gabriel Borkman* going?"

"Exhaustingly!" Myra switched moods immediately and became intensely, volubly, professional. "You know, Ibsen is *the* most exhausting writer. You can never relax into him as the run proceeds. I noticed it with *Rosmersholm,* and I'm finding it with *Borkman,* too. Even with Shakespeare, when the play is well run in, you can coast along, to some extent. Not with Ibsen. You have to be on the *qui vive* the *whole* time. Darlings, the *sweat* at the end of the performance . . ."

She was no longer talking to family but to a stage crowd. The new impulse, or new mood, took them through the pudding—though Myra, who had to be careful of her figure and really didn't care what she ate, waved aside the plum duff or syllabub and toyed with cheese and biscuits. She talked about the National Theatre, the forthcoming change of director, and what she had said to the director-elect, and around and around the theatrical maypole. Cordelia threw in questions, Granville made appropriate responses, Pat kept amiably silent. It would have looked, to an outsider, like a pretty typical two-generation family party.

It was about ten to eight by the clock behind her when Myra pushed away her coffee cup.

"Right. I don't know what you men are going to do, but Cordelia and I have something to discuss. Alone."

8

"Now," said Myra, closing the bedroom door behind her.

She gestured toward the double bed, but Cordelia, with apparent composure, walked around it and sat on the upright chair at the dressing table. She looked up at her mother expectantly.

"What do you think you're doing?" demanded Myra.

Cordelia furrowed her brow. "Sorry—what are we actually talking about?"

Myra's mouth was twisted. "We are talking about this book you are telling everyone you are writing about me."

"Oh, yes . . . what was your question?"

Myra's voice rose a couple of tones toward hysteria. "I want to know what you are damned well writing!"

Cordelia nodded, apparently with unruffled composure. "Well, the bulk of the book will be a survey of your career—plays, films, television plays—in chronological order. There will be extracts from your notices—you know I've always kept your scrapbooks—and personal reactions, for example from other actors, perhaps from writers, from any theatrical notables who saw you and will talk to me. And of course I've seen everything you've done since the late sixties."

"I know all about that side. I've talked to your damned publishers."

Cordelia was irritatingly nannyish. "There, then. What's all the fuss about?"

"What *else* is there? They say there's supposed to be some kind of personal memoir."

"That's right. The fans will want to get some kind of picture of what the Dame Myra they admire is like as a person. Who better to write it than me?"

A nerve in Myra's cheek twitched. Anybody seeing her now for the first time might have been forgiven for thinking she was rather an ugly woman. "What are you writing?"

Cordelia shrugged. "Oh, I've hardly begun that section yet."

"What are you intending to write? Or, to put it another way, why are you here?"

"Surely that's obvious?" The nannyish tone was still there. Clearly Cordelia knew it was effective. "Ben Cotterel and all the material about him are here. Not to mention his son and daughter-in-law, who've been very helpful and put everything at my disposal. For a daughter writing about her mother, the natural approach to the subject is through the father—through the question of how she came into the world."

"You sly little bitch! You will write nothing about me and Ben. Nothing! I will not have that old business raked through again. I've told Maxim's, your publishers, that I must have absolute right of veto on anything you write."

"Oh? And what did they say to that?"

Myra glared and changed the subject. "What else are you intending to write about?"

"Really I haven't decided. I tell you, I've hardly begun work on that section yet. It's difficult because there's such an embarrassment of riches." She leaned forward, throwing aside the mask of coolness and competence for one of long-nurtured grievance. "Shall I write about Louis? He's dead, so I can. Shall I tell your fans what he did to me over the year you were married to him? And shall I tell them how you stood aside and never intervened—because you rather liked him doing it to me? What shall I tell them about

Digby, your second? That association had a certain tragi-
comic flavor to it, which might come across well. People
always like laughing at the great—the appeal of the banana
skin. Shall I tell them about Mark and Harold and young
Dale? Shall I give a paragraph or two each to poor old
Winston, Murray, James, Gabriel—?"

"Bitch! You haven't got a hope of publishing. They're all
alive except Winston."

"They'll die," said Cordelia, sitting back in her chair and
resuming her calm stance. Myra roamed around the room
like a stage tigress, rubbing her hands.

"What have I done to be treated like this?"

"That's a good question," said Cordelia. "Perhaps I won't
concentrate on husbands and lovers. Perhaps I'll tell them
how you locked me in your costume trunk and left me crying and screaming for an hour while you made love to Murray. That *was* Murray, wasn't it? Shall I tell them of all the
schools you sent me away to and all the scenes you made
there before you took me out of them? Shall I tell them the
things you used to say to me when I was going through
adolescence: how I'd never be a beauty, never get a husband,
always be a useless, spotty lump. That was your exact
phrase, I remember. They'll want to know about all the
scenes, all the rages, the outrageous performances at every
emotional crisis of your life. They expect that sort of thing
from the acting profession. And of course I'll tell them how
the rages were vented on me: how you've sneered at me in
public, called me stupid, plain, frigid, robbed me of every
shred of self-confidence I had, and broken up all my pathetic
little romances."

"That's nonsense. I never have."

Cordelia turned on her with narrowed eyes. "Don't lie in
private, lie in public, Mother. You know, and I know, how
it's been. Now I've broken away from you, I can see it
clearer than ever."

"I have one consolation—one consolation," said Myra,
raising her eyes to heaven as if suddenly transplanted into a
mid-Victorian weepie. "None of this is publishable."

"Oh, but the Ben episode will come out," said Cordelia, smiling complacently. "The private life of an actress is maybe not of *that* much interest, except to the sensation press. But Ben was a great writer. Most of your others have been nonentities, like Granville, but Ben was great. People are going to write biographies of Ben whether you like it or not. You don't imagine they are going to ignore the affair with you, do you? Anyway, I certainly shan't. In fact, it's going to be central to my book, the opening episode. It illustrates so beautifully the essence of your emotional life: the way you sail into affairs, because you see some glory or some advantage to yourself, and then fall flat on your face and get lumbered with the consequences. Notably me. I'm one of the consequences you got lumbered with, and you've never forgiven me."

"You won't be able to publish any of this, you know."

"You'll die," said Cordelia without compassion. "You'll grow old and terrible and lonely, but eventually you'll die. Then I shall publish."

Myra underwent one of her rapid changes of mood, and her voice took on a wheedling tone. "You've got it all wrong, you know. The story of my affair with Ben. You've never let me tell my side."

"Oh, I know your side of the story. I've read it in the *News of the World* for September 1963. Though your account was not very accurate. In fact, it was a tissue of lies."

"It was not!"

"You rearrange the facts to suit your view of yourself. I know the facts because I've read the letters."

"You scrubby little muckraker! You've been reading my letters to Ben!"

"I have. No wonder he tired of you so quickly. I've never seen such a prolonged howl of egotism."

"You don't know the provocation! You don't know what he did to me, the things he said. You've only read one side of it."

"That's where you're wrong, Mother. Pat and I went down to Pelstock yesterday."

"*What?* . . . You're lying. Minnie would never have let you in."

"Sunday is Minnie's day off, remember? I still have my key to the house. I thought the letters would be in the safe, and I thought I knew the combination number. I've stood at that door often enough, watching you open it to get out jewelry or the little treasures you've got stashed away there. As a child I always used to wonder if there were relics of my father there. And there were! We took them and photo-copied them at Pat's school. So now they're part of the archive."

Myra's face was red and blotchy, her eyes bulbous. "Thief! Traitor!"

"You can only be a traitor where loyalty's due. You gave me no love, no protection, no security. I tried for years to love you, then to admire you, but I never could. You gave me no reason to. That's why I've always clung to the idea of my father—"

"Your father! That cold, old lecher."

"Oh, I can see now that he was not perfect. I think you're right: He was cold, and probably selfish, too. He capitalized on his affair with you to make one more novel when his inspiration had been waning for years. But he had dignity, he didn't lie, and he tried to do his duty by me—to support me, if not protect me. Basically he was an honest person."

"He was a snake! He exploited me!"

"No, Mother, it was you who was the exploiter. If he capitalized on the affair, that's because he knew perfectly well that *you* were exploiting *him*—sleeping with him, having his child, for the kudos, and for the play you hoped to screw out of him. He was not a gentleman, maybe, but he was not a dishonorable man. I was right to cling to the idea of my father."

There was a moment's silence, and then Myra's face assumed an ugly sneer.

"If he is, in fact, your father."

Cordelia flinched. "What?"

"If that bundle of senility is in fact your father."

"I know Ben Cotterel is my father! I even know when I was conceived. It was that weekend you came down from Glasgow, when you were playing in *Earnest.*"

Myra shrugged, smiling dangerously. "Looking at you— so lumpish and stupid—I've always thought your father was probably the Cameron Highlander I had it off with in the train loo on the journey down."

Cordelia threw herself out of her chair and at her mother, her hands on her throat.

"You're trying to rob me of my father! You monster! You monster!" she screamed.

Cordelia got back to the Rectory at about half past ten. She didn't go straight down to the tent, but let herself in at the front door—as she had been encouraged to do when she came up to work during the day—and knocked at the door of the sitting room, where Roderick and Caroline were watching the news.

"Hello," said Caroline, turning the television off. "You're late. I think Pat's down in the tent. Did it go well?"

"What? Oh, the meeting with my mother. It went pretty much as I expected. . . . Well, I suppose rather worse. I was intending to keep very cool."

"Oh, dear. And you didn't?"

"No, I . . . blew up. Just the sort of scene Myra loves."

"How did that happen? Was it something she said?"

"Yes. She said— Oh, never mind. I've been walking it off since. I've cooled down now. I realize it was just something she made up simply to get me to blow my top. I should have known she'd do that when things weren't going her way. I was a fool to let her succeed."

"Is there any chance of making things up?" asked Roderick. "Any use my volunteering as a peacemaker?"

Cordelia's fingers began working nervously at the head-scarf she had taken off as she came in.

"None at all, I should think. Unless— Oh, never mind. Just an idea that occurred to me. . . . But there's really no point in trying to be a peacemaker. Mother belongs to a part of my life that's over. Thank God. I want to get the book written, and when it is, I won't much care what happens to it. I'll put one copy in a strongbox and let the publishers and lawyers fight over the text. Maybe they'll just publish the bit about her career. Maybe they can salvage something from the other part. I shan't care much. It will at least exist, and one day someone will read it. I will have got it out of my system."

"And you can get on with your life," said Caroline quietly.

"That's right. Maybe make a career in journalism, maybe have a family—who knows, maybe both. Myra will be a part of my past. I didn't want her to come here. I'll be glad if I never see her again."

"Perhaps that would be wise," said Caroline. "Sad, but wise. Do you really have to write this book?"

"I think so." Cordelia paused and darted a sharp look at them both. "Unless . . ."

"Yes?"

"Well, I've thought over the past few days, when I've realized what a lot of marvelous material there is here, that what I'd really like to do is write a biography of my father. The authorized biography."

Roderick and Cordelia looked at her, startled.

"This is a new idea," said Roderick at last.

"Yes. But I can't see there's anything against it, and there are all sorts of things in its favor. I could tell my mother I'd given up the book on her. . . ."

Roderick screwed up his face. "Of course we've always realized that eventually something of the sort will be written and that in all probability we will have to cooperate—probably, as the heirs, even nominate someone to write it."

"Well, then."

"But you see the fact that father is so popular and well-thought-of means that there are all sorts of people queuing up to write it. In America there's even a Benedict Cotterel Society, which writes to us about all sorts of things, from changes in the manuscripts to what brands of underwear he wore. Soon the BBC is going to serialize *The Silver Sky* on television, and that will only increase his popularity. Already there are lots of academics, here and overseas, who have written books on *his* books. Many of them are itching to be asked to write his life."

"But I wrote my M.A. on him! I've been in love with his books since I was in my early teens."

Roderick shook his head and became, Caroline thought, horribly schoolmasterish.

"I don't want to be rude, Cordelia, but that is at a rather different level. These are people with solid academic backgrounds, research qualifications. Inevitably we'll think first of one of them when it comes to picking a biographer. As you know, there are episodes in Father's life—probably more than you realize—that need to be treated with great discretion; honestly, I hope, but still circumspectly."

"I get you," said Cordelia with more than a trace of bitterness. "You think I'll be too sensational. Play up the love affairs to get the book serialized in the Sunday papers."

"No, no, I'm sure you wouldn't," said Roderick hurriedly. "I know you have too much respect for your father to do that. But inevitably an older, more experienced writer would have more of the necessary weapons. Tact and discretion don't come naturally to the young. You acquire them over the years."

"And however discreet you were, there would still be something sensational in the situation itself," Caroline pointed out. "A natural daughter writing the life of her father. It's just made for the Sundays. Inevitably you'd have to write about the affair between Ben and your mother."

"Oh, yes," said Cordelia.

"There you are. Even if you did it very discreetly—and to be frank, I don't think you're inclined to do that—it would be seized on."

"I think you're being very unfair," said Cordelia. "I'm the best-qualified person to write it because I *am* involved, he *is* part of me. . . . I love him, and always have since I knew about him."

"From one point of view that's exactly what disqualifies you," said Roderick.

"Anyway, I don't see any point in our having this conversation *now*," said Caroline, getting up in the hope of putting an end to it. "Whoever we choose—an American academic, a British one, a professional biographer, you—we aren't going to do it now. To me there's something distasteful just in talking about it. I'm sure I mentioned to you earlier that we have no intention of doing anything about a biographer until such time as Ben dies."

Cordelia came up close to Caroline and looked into her eyes.

"Oh, but he is dead, isn't he?" she said.

Into the silence that followed there intruded the siren of an approaching police car.

9

After Cordelia and Myra had disappeared upstairs in the
Red Lion to have their "discussion," the men of the party
had trooped through the dining room and back toward the
bar.

"Best thing is to have a drink and wait," said Granville
Ashe to Pat. "My guess is, there'll be a big bust-up, and then
the peace processes can begin. Anyway, the thing's out of
our hands."

It was, of course. Pat's instinct was to head back to the
Rectory and have a read while the light was still good.
Granville Ashe had not seemed to him a particularly interesting person on their brief acquaintanceship. But then, anybody in the shadow of Myra Mason was likely to pale. He
himself had probably not said more than fifty words during
the evening thus far. He would give Granville the benefit of
the doubt.

"Fine," he said with his slow smile. "Just a pint, and then
I'll be cutting off home."

The bar was less crowded than it had been before dinner.
The Red Lion at Maudsley attracted a healthy rather than a
drinking clientele. Many of the resident guests were probably taking an evening stroll down the cliffs to the beach or
observing wildlife on the Downs. There were a great number

of bird-watchers among the people who booked in there summer after summer. Pat bought the drinks and, observing that Roderick Cotterel's sister was already at the bar, steered Granville in the opposite direction. Pat recognized poison when he saw it. Granville came to rest at an empty table beside Commodore and Daisy Critchley. Unfortunately, the commodore did not seem disposed to regard the tables as separate.

"Ah, the ladies have gone for a chat, have they?" he said with that geniality that Caroline found suspect. "Mother-and-daughter talk, I suppose."

"That's right," said Granville. "Mother-and-daughter talk."

Pat had hoped that Granville might freeze them out, but he seemed inclined to be friendly, no doubt to make up for Myra's frostiness earlier in the evening. He smiled at them, a not-very-interesting-leading-man-in-a-not-very-interesting-play sort of smile.

"You're an actor, too, aren't you?" asked Daisy Critchley with a quick stretching of her mouth.

"Oh, a very humble one," said Granville with practiced self-deprecation and sipping his beer. "Or, if not humble, lowly. A born spear-carrier, I'm afraid. Made to swell a progress, start a scene or two." He saw that he had lost them. "My lot is mostly endless tours of the provinces," he explained, "though of course one mustn't call them that these days. When the West End plays go on tour, they tend to call on me to replace the star who's gone off to make a television series. Or one may come to rest with some repertory company in Leatherhead or Guildford. That's what I've been doing for the past six months."

It was an opening into theatrical gossip, and one the Critchleys were certain to take up. After a time Pat shut out the talk and looked around the room. He was on the long seat under the window, and he had an excellent view. Now that the bar was less crowded, he had a view of individuals, not just of one seething mass. Some of the people standing or sitting with their drinks he already knew, for he and Cordelia had been here often enough in the evening: There was the Maudsley greengrocer, there was the man from the post office, and over there was the family he had talked to on the beach. The woman reading he had seen before somewhere, and there, centrally situated, was that sister of Roderick's whom he had just avoided. She had a table to herself now. Odd woman. Unsettling, somehow. When she had come up to them at dinner, there had been a mixture of hostility and obsequiousness that Pat—with his young man's freshness of vision—found difficult to account for.

Now Isobel was clearly nervous. "Cat on a hot tin roof" was the phrase that sprang to Pat's mind. She fumbled when she put a cigarette into her little gold holder; she smoked a few puffs, then extinguished it and ejected it into the ashtray. She started up from her table, then thought better of it and settled back again, crossing and uncrossing her legs. What's she got to be nervous about? wondered Pat. He decided that she was someone he and Cordelia would have as little to do with as possible, the sort he found quite insufferable: overdressed, neurotic, discontented. How odd that she should be so different from Roderick. The Cotterels had been good to Cordelia—and good *for* her, too. This one, if she got her claws into her half sister, could spread her neuroticism like a small plague.

Isobel made a decision: She got up and marched over to the door that led to the back sections of the Red Lion—to the lavatories, the kitchens and dining room, and the stairs leading up to the guests' bedrooms. No doubt she was going to fetch something from her room. She had left a filmy scarf on her table to reserve it.

Pat turned his attention back to the conversation.

"Yes, we are newly married—" Granville was saying.

"Congratulations!" said Daisy Critchley. "Of course we saw it in the *Telegraph*."

"Thanks. But in fact we're . . . friends from way back. It must be—oh, ten, twelve years ago when we met; at Stratford, when I played Fortinbras to her Gertrude."

It was an odd way of putting it, Pat thought. Perhaps

Granville Ashe thought he could rely on the Critchleys' having only the vaguest notions of the importance of the various roles in *Hamlet*. And probably he was right.

"I decided then that Myra was the greatest actress I was ever likely to appear with. And so it has proved. Not that I haven't been in plays with wonderful women—some of them pure magic. Even an unknown like me gets breaks sometimes! But none of them has had the presence, the command, the sheer aura of Myra on stage. Critics would agree. I don't see her Gertrude being equaled in my lifetime."

Pat had heard quite a lot of this sort of thing in the last few months, and his attention span was accordingly small. His mind wandered. He saw that Isobel had returned to the Saloon Bar. She seemed still more highly strung than before. She bought herself another drink from the landlord at the bar, took it to her table, sipped it, then rummaged in her handbag. Then—apparently having forgotten something upstairs or on the pretense of having forgotten something—she got up again and made for the door leading to the lavatories and the guests' bedrooms.

"How did you meet up with Dame Myra again, then?" Commodore Critchley was prodding Granville.

"Oh, that's simple. Myra's at the National at the moment. I'm sure you know the system there: lots of plays playing in repertory. That means you may be in *John Gabriel Borkman* for three or four nights, then have several days off. Days off don't exactly suit Myra. She's an actress first, last, and all stops in between. She has a one-woman show that she takes around the country. It's called *A Room of My Own*, and it's about women writers: Jane Austen, Charlotte Brontë, Katherine Mansfield, Virginia Woolf. Letters, extracts from diaries, and so on. She doesn't exactly *do* them, or anything like that, so the show can be done from a suitcase. Not really my cup of tea, but a damned fine evening even so. Anyway, she brought it down to Guildford for a Sunday evening performance, and that was that."

"Guildford's where you've been acting, is it?" asked Daisy Critchley. She asked it guilelessly, but Pat felt sure it was with malicious intent. Thus did Noel Coward dismiss Norfolk.

"That's right." Granville Ashe smiled ruefully. "Not the middle of the theatrical universe, but it means even a very minor luminary like myself can get good parts there. Since the beginning of the year I've done Benedick, Teddy in *The Homecoming*, and we've just finished *Noises Off*. There are some compensations, I assure you, about Guildford."

"Oh, please, I wasn't—"

But Daisy Critchley was interrupted. Isobel Allick had hurried back into the Saloon Bar, and this time she came straight over to them. Her manner was nervous, but also— Pat was sure of it—excited. As if she got what she had hoped for and intended to make the most of it. She addressed herself to Granville Ashe and Pat, her mouth working convulsively.

"Oh, Mr. Ashe, and—I'm sorry, I don't know your name. I thought you ought to know. I had to go upstairs a little while ago, to . . . to fetch a handkerchief, and there were these very loud voices coming from your wife's room. Well, not to mince matters, a row. And I've just had to go up again for—well, actually, I was worried, because Cordelia *is* my sister, in a way, and I just *hoped* she wasn't going to do anything foolish—and in fact there were sounds of . . . of violence. I mean they were actually physically *fighting*."

Her voice faded away. Both the Critchleys were looking up at her with naked, avid interest. But Granville Ashe put a restraining hand on Pat's arm and smiled his young-leading-man's smile up at her.

"Thanks you for telling us, Mrs. . . . er . . . I'm sure you are concerned, but really you don't have to be. I've seen plenty of women fighting during my time in the theater. They may make a lot of noise, but I can assure you they never do each other any real harm. It's like women's tennis; it just doesn't have the ferocity of men's. Just relax. We knew there were likely to be difficulties. This sounds worse than it is. There's no cause to be alarmed."

There was a moment's silence. Isobel couldn't think what to say.

"Well, I hope you're right."

The remark came out flatly. Isobel had obviously expected to cause a great sensation. She went back to her table, took a discontented swill at her drink, and sat back, looking at the ceiling. Then Pat saw a thought occurring to her, and she leaned over sideways and conversed in low tones with the woman reading Drabble.

Granville Ashe had kept his hand on Pat's arm.

"I meant what I said to that interfering bitch. It *is* much less worse than it sounds, always. If one of us goes up and tries to intervene, we'll just fan the flames—*and* get caught in the middle, to boot. It will work itself out quite quickly, you'll see. Probably Cordelia will flounce off, they'll both feel they've won, and the whole thing will just go off the boil. This is just women's nonsense. Much better we don't interfere."

The way Granville put it rather shocked Pat. You didn't talk in those terms in his circles. Clearly the women's movement had had little effect on the world of provincial rep. He wondered if Granville was right. This was surely something more than a mere backstage brawl. There were real issues here, and real hatred. Hatred, Pat suspected, on both sides. Myra was a formidable personality, determined to have her way, and Cordelia was large physically. There lurked in him the fear that they could do each other real harm. On the other hand, was a final, violent explosion just what the relationship needed? Would it purge each from the other's system, finally and beneficially? Pat was a peaceful soul but not a pacifist. He believed that some long-festering emotions find in violence their healthiest outlet. Perhaps that would be the case here.

He sat on, irresolute. Around him the talk had turned back to theater. The landlord, going on his rounds collecting glasses, had paused to listen. Names were being shamelessly dropped by Granville. Pat slipped out of his seat and went toward the door leading to the loos.

As he went through it, the back door to the pub banged shut. He nearly darted over to open it, to see who had gone out, but then he restrained the urge. If it was Cordelia who had just gone out, he thought, she would certainly need time to recover herself emotionally. He stood against the door. To his right was a door marked PRIVATE; that, he knew, led to the landlord's quarters. To his left was a passageway leading to the ladies' and gentlemen's lavatories, and beyond that to the kitchens and the dining room, which also had a more acceptable entrance on the other side of the bar. Ahead of him was the staircase leading to the guests' bedrooms.

Pat stood at the foot of the stairs, listening. He felt an intruder. There was a notice suspended from the ceiling saying HOTEL GUESTS ONLY. He could hear no sounds of conflict. From a distant room he could hear a transistor radio; that was all. He darted up the stairs and stopped four or five steps from the top. The corridor, with the doors to ten or twelve guest bedrooms, was deserted. Pat had seen Myra's room key on the table at dinner. It was Room 3. The door with that number on was quite near the head of the stairs. It stared back at him. Behind it, all was quiet—neither voices nor sounds of struggle. Pat sighed with relief. Apparently the fight was over.

When he got back to the bar, the circle around Granville had been augmented. The landlord had sat down, the man from the post office had come over and stood near, and people from other tables were listening in.

"Oh, yes, I've acted with Judi Dench," Granville was saying. "An absolute sweetie."

Pat looked at his glass of beer. There was only a quarter of an inch left in it. He'd leave them all to it. He slipped toward the Saloon Bar door and out into the twilight. Then he walked toward the Volkswagen, parked around the side.

Granville Ashe was rather enjoying himself. It is true that if he had announced himself in the Saloon Bar of the Red Lion as an actor, he would in any case have been the object of interest and curiosity. That had always been his experience, gained in bars up and down the country. Still, it was

certainly also true that being Dame Myra Mason's husband
meant that the interest was sharpened, became more personal. His wide-ranging anecdotes were enjoyed, but someone eventually always brought the conversation back to
Myra. If questioned, Granville replied gallantly but un-
revealingly and directed the conversation off in another direction. The perfect stage gentleman.

Granville dropped names, but he did not only drop
names; he had a fund of theatrical disasters, of coincidences
and premonitions, traditions and superstitions. He had just
finished *Noises Off,* itself the story of accumulating theatrical disaster. One or two of his listeners had seen it, and he
could direct his stories at them.

"You remember in Act Two, after the business with the
axe, when Dottie's tied my shoelaces together and I sort of
hop onstage—of course we're backstage at this point—well,
as I went through the bedroom door . . ."

Granville was a good raconteur. He made the story vivid
even to those who hadn't seen the play.

"And even though the play is *about* disasters onstage, if
you actually *have* one that isn't in the script, it has dreadful
consequences, because everything is so carefully organized
and timed. God knows if anyone in the audience realized it,
but there were one or two onstage that were close to heart
attacks that night, I can tell you."

His audience laughed easily. He had put them at ease.
Now he was in full flood.

"Plays *about* the theater are always hell to do. You have
to make a distinction between the characters' theatricality
on stage and *off* stage. I remember once when I was in *Trelawny of the Wells* at Bristol—"

He was interrupted by a loud report. A sharp, split-sec-
ond bang. Everyone around the two tables jumped in the air,
but Granville was the first to laugh.

"Golly—you should have seen yourselves. Must be some
old banger going by. Probably my new stepdaughter and her
boyfriend, if what I hear is true. Good that those spoilsports
at the Ministry of Transport allow a few old crates on the

roads still. What was I talking about? Oh, yes, *Trelawny of the Wells*. Well, there was this young actress, and between you and me there wasn't a lot of talent there, or a lot between the ears, and the producer was getting pretty frayed around the edges trying to drum things into her, and the more he went on at this pretty little thing with the tiny brain, the more she turned to jelly, so that before long she was reduced to three or four stock movements, and her voice had become a squeak of panic. Well, two or three of us saw what was happening, and we decided—"

"Excuse me, Mr.—"

He had been interrupted again. It was the woman who had been reading Margaret Drabble. An English gentlewoman—in jumper and skirt, pearls around her neck, and discreetly made up. She seemed painfully shy in this situation, but insistent, as if doing a duty. Granville smiled charmingly.

"Yes?"

"I don't like to interrupt, but that shot—"

"Oh!" Granville's face cleared with enlightenment. "That wasn't a shot. Just an old banger passing down the road."

"No." She stuck to her guns. "I was—well, I was in the loo. I'm sure I could hear much better than you in here. It was a shot, and it came from directly over my head."

"Oh, I'm sure you're mistaken."

"Mr.—er—"

"Ashe."

"Mr. Ashe, my husband was an architect, and I have a very good sense of the geography of buildings. I'm sure that the room directly above the ladies' lavatory is your wife's room."

Her very shyness made her urgency impressive. The bar was quiet now, and people had come over to listen. Granville looked into the sea of faces. Standing out was Isobel's— hungry, excited, a little drunk. About all the faces there was a voracious quality that was disturbing. Granville paused, irresolute.

"I'm sure you're wrong. But perhaps I'd better just go up and see—"

"*Please* do."

The scene had taken on the quality of one of those theatrical occasions that Granville had been talking about. He felt surrounded by a tense, watchful, wolfish crowd. He tried to defuse the situation by being conspicuously casual.

"Keep my place," he said. "I'll just nip up and poke my head around the door."

But it was the measure of the woman's convincingness that as he walked through the door leading into the back part of the Red Lion, they all, quietly, surged toward it. Someone—it was the commodore—held the door open a little so that they could hear. They heard footsteps, not hurrying, going up the stairs. Straining, they heard him quietly turn the doorknob. Then, after a moment, they heard the click of the light switch.

There was a moment's silence.

Then they heard his feet running, stumbling down the stairs, and he broke into the bar, his face ashen.

"Get the police! Ring for the police! Myra's been shot!"

10

In the police car taking her to Cottingham, Cordelia was very quiet. Cottingham was the nearest town of any size, and it was a journey of ten miles or so. Occasionally she looked out at the darkened landscape, now merely a rolling, lowering mass, but mostly she sat silently gazing down at her hands, nervously working in her lap. The fact was, she was ashamed.

The policemen had come straight to the front door of the Rectory and had asked for her by name. Roderick had brought them into the sitting room, and the senior man had introduced himself as Chief Inspector Meredith and the younger one as Sergeant Flood. The inspector had said that he was sorry to have to tell her that her mother was dead, and Cordelia had said, "Dead?" in the manner of second-rate plays—so often a better mirror of life than good ones. The inspector had asked if it was true that Cordelia had been at the Red Lion earlier in the evening and then if it was true that she had had a quarrel with her mother. When Cordelia had nodded, unhesitatingly, he had asked her to come over to the station at Cottingham for questioning. Cordelia, who had shown no emotion beyond surprise at the death of her mother, immediately agreed.

Chief Inspector Meredith had also asked her to bring a

nightdress and basic toilet requirements. That augured ill,
thought Roderick and Caroline, but Cordelia had merely
said she would fetch them from the tent. Meredith had not
allowed this, nor would he let Roderick or Caroline go and
get them. Sergeant Flood had gone down the lawn, and they
had all stood around waiting for him to return, in an awkward silence broken only by Meredith's murmurs of apol-
ogy. Pat, in pajamas, was with Flood when he came back,
but Cordelia was allowed only to kiss him briefly before she
was hustled into the police car and driven away.

"Don't worry, I didn't do it," she had called.

No one, at that point, had said anything about murder,
but they hadn't needed to.

Now, speeding in the car toward Cottingham, there was
something in the quality of Cordelia's silence that puzzled
Inspector Meredith. He was aware that there was no grief
there. Cordelia had pretended to none, and none was perhaps to be expected, from the little he had heard about the
relationship from the dead woman's husband. He had had a
very sketchy talk with Granville Ashe while the technical
experts and the police doctor had been taking over the Red
Lion and getting down to their routine business with the
body. But, sitting next to Cordelia in the backseat of the car,
Meredith got the odd idea that Cordelia was not thinking
about the death of her mother at all. He had had a distinct
sense of tension, of something unspoken, between her and
the Cotterels, and he wondered if it was that that she was
thinking of.

He shook off the idea. He was fancying things.

Soon they came to a landscape of bright shop windows
and traffic lights. When they drove up at Cottingham Police
Station, Cordelia got out of the car quite naturally and stood
waiting for the policemen to escort her into the building.
While she stood there, a flashbulb went off. The press—
albeit only a local stringer, harbinger of the metropolitan
hordes—were already on to the story. Cordelia did not react
in any way. She was all too used to being photographed,
usually with Myra; throughout her childhood she had got-

ten used to dressing up for the press men—usually in clothes that suggested she was rather younger than she actually was. Meredith and Flood closed in behind her, and she allowed herself to be shunted gently into the station.

It was an old building, built on to accommodate the increase in crime, or paperwork. She waited, along with a drunk and distraught mother, while Meredith consulted with the duty sergeant about a vacant interview room. She let them lead her down painted brick corridors to a cheerless, bare room with green-painted walls, one high window, and a table and three chairs. Flood took his chair some way apart, flipped his notebook open to a clean page, and began to take notes. Cordelia took the chair on the side of the table, which left her with her back to the door, and sat down without fuss, looking calmly at Meredith.

"I thought we'd begin tonight, but if you're tired or confused, just tell me, and we'll break off," he said.

Cordelia nodded. He had a nice voice, the slight Welshness giving it a strong hint of music, of remoteness. Altogether he was a reassuring rather than an unsettling presence, for he looked calm, methodical, and unlikely to make mistakes. He was square, stocky, with a kindly face—probably a good father who had played with his children a lot when they were little, watched them at school sports, enjoyed Saturday evenings with his wife in a pub when he was off duty. Cordelia wondered what it was like to have had a good father.

Meredith had taken the chair on the other side of the table. Now he began clearing his throat.

"Let's get the facts straight first. You agreed you were at the Red Lion in Maudsley earlier this evening and that you went up to the bedroom with your mother and that there you had a quarrel." Cordelia nodded. "What was the quarrel about?"

"My life," said Cordelia. Then she pulled herself together. "No, I don't want to be melodramatic. It's quite simple. I've signed a contract with Maxim's, the publishers, to write a

book about my mother. It will be a survey of her acting
career. . . ."

"Yes?" Meredith raised an eyebrow.

"And a more . . . personal section. It was this that
caused the trouble. There are—there *were*—many things in
my mother's life that she didn't want discussed."

"But which you intended to discuss?"

"Yes."

Meredith thought for a moment that Cordelia was going
to elaborate on this, but she fell silent.

"A moment ago you said the quarrel was about your life,"
Meredith said gently. "Pardon me if I'm putting it insensi-
tively, but is this book a sort of revenge—revenge for the
upbringing you had?"

Cordelia gazed ahead thoughtfully, then sighed. "Yes
. . . I suppose I would have put it another way myself, but
that's about it."

"You showed no surprise at the idea that your mother had
been murdered—in fact, you assumed it before I told you
so."

"She was the sort of woman whom many people would
want to kill."

"So the thrust of your book about her would have been:
marvelous actress, terrible person?"

"Well, that is pretty much the truth about Myra."

"What is it exactly you have to complain of?"

An air of weariness came over Cordelia. "Neglect, a succession of men, constant abuse and ridicule—"

"Physical brutality?"

"From Myra? Now and then, I suppose. Hairbrush
spanking and that sort of thing. That's not important. That
sort of pain doesn't last. It's the constant, daily pain for a
child of looking to her mother for love and knowing she's
nothing to her—a burden, a reminder, something to jeer at
or to cuddle for the cameras if the newsmen come. . . .
This isn't what I was going to put in the book, by the way."

"No?"

"It would have sounded too much like whining. The reviewers would have said that all theatrical children get neglected, all actors and actresses have giant egos, and most remarkable people have poor-spirited children who resent them. I can just hear what they would say. They would have let Myra off the hook. . . . I was going to go about it in a more subtle way."

"What way was that?"

Cordelia leaned forward, now really interested, creatively interested, in what she was saying.

"The more I looked at it—having got away from her at last—the more I saw there was a pattern in her emotional life. She would sail into relationships—for selfish reasons, always, for pure sensual gratification or career advancement or whatever—and then find herself horribly encumbered by the consequences, usually because she had no understanding of other people. It was rather comic, really, or could have been told in a comic way. Myra could never bear to be laughed at."

"You thought making her a comic butt was a better revenge than making her look a monster?"

"Well . . . yes."

"Could you give me an example of her tendency to land herself in the soup?"

Cordelia thought. "Well, there was Louis, her first husband. Louis Leconte. She went into that for pure sexual gratification. Louis was a French diplomat and a complete all-round sensualist. He was also a sadist. That turned out to be one of his main forms of sexual gratification."

"Was this sadism vented on your mother or on you?"

"On me, first."

"Was there sexual abuse or just physical brutality?"

"Both. Mother didn't know about the sexual abuse. Not then."

"But she knew about the brutality?"

"Yes. She knew."

"What did she do about it?"

"She sat back and enjoyed it. No, that was unfair. She stood aside. She took up an attitude of conspicuous unconcern. But I suspect now that she rather enjoyed it. Louis went further than she ever dared to do."

"I see." Meredith sighed. He didn't want to ask the next question. "How old were you?"

"I was eight."

"How long did this go on?"

"About a year. Eventually, Louis turned the brutality on her. That was inevitable, I suppose, because my mother was intolerable to live with, even for quite nice men, and Louis certainly wasn't that. She would arrive for performances with cuts and bruises. She had to weigh the sensual side, which was marvelous, or so she has told me over and over again since, against something which she did not like at all. It was quite a struggle for a while, but eventually she saw sense and sent him packing. It was quite the most spectacular of her breakups. Mostly they went quietly, on a wing and a prayer of thanksgiving."

"Where is this Louis Leconte now?" asked Meredith, his interest quickened.

"In Père Lachaise. One of his later lovers killed him. . . . She got a very light sentence."

"I see," said Meredith regretfully.

He thought for a moment, and Cordelia, too, seemed submerged in memory.

"So that was how you were going to treat her, and that was what the row was all about."

"Yes."

"Could you have published?"

"Perhaps not. But a book *exists*, even if it's not published. You know, like Chatterton's poetry, or Hopkins's. I was going to lodge it with a bank."

"And it could have been published after her death?"

Cordelia saw the trap.

"After her death, and that of most of the other people involved."

She shot him a smile that said: Don't take me for a fool. Meredith shifted in his chair.

"Point taken. Now can we get back to this row with your mother?"

"It was she who wanted the row. Or at least she wanted the book idea firmly trodden on, and she couldn't think of any other way but bullying to accomplish it. I didn't want any row. I've grown away from her. She's irrelevant to me."

Meredith could see, as plain as plain, that that was not true.

"I see," he said noncommittally. "Now, how long did this quarrel last? When did you both go to your mother's bedroom, and when did you leave it?"

"I really don't know . . . Wait. We went up there after dinner. Mother looked at her watch and said we two had something to discuss and the men could do what they wanted. I looked at the clock in the dining room at the same time. I don't know if it was right, but it said about a quarter or ten to eight."

"And when you left the bedroom?"

"I haven't the faintest idea. We'd just had a row. You don't look at your watch in those circumstances."

"I suppose not. But when you left, your mother was still alive?"

"Of course she was. Very much so. Livid with rage."

"What did you do after you left her room?"

"Went out of the Red Lion by the back entrance. Then I walked it off."

"Where?"

"On the cliffs for a bit. Then I walked down to the beach. The sea is very soothing."

"Did anybody see you?"

"I don't know . . . I think there were one or two people on the beach. When it began to get really dark, I walked up again and took the road to the Rectory."

"And you never went back to the Red Lion or to your mother's room?"

"No. I never wanted to see her again."

Meredith shifted in his chair. Cordelia had the air of an honest witness. Almost too honest for her own good.

"Tell me—one of the witnesses from the Red Lion, hearing the row from outside in the corridor, said that it actually involved physical violence. Is that so?"

Cordelia looked down at her lap. Her hands were once more doing that intricate working together, as if she were doing crochet work without needles or thread.

"Yes . . . That was bad, wasn't it? I went in intending to stay perfectly cool, and then I let that happen."

"Why did it?"

"She knows how to needle me. Myra certainly understood that." Meredith waited, and eventually Cordelia said: "It was something silly she said about my father. She knows she can needle me by talking about my father."

Meredith nodded. He was old enough to remember, dimly, the fuss in the gutter newspapers about pretty little Myra Mason's baby by the elderly novelist. It had been, he would guess, in the early sixties—just one scandal in the era of scandals.

"Ah, yes, tell me about that, will you? Your father is Ben Cotterel, isn't he?"

"That's right," said Cordelia quickly.

"Who lives at the Rectory, where I . . . came for you tonight."

"Roderick is his son. Pat and I are camping on the lawn."

"I believe I've heard that the old man is . . . not what he was."

"Yes. I went up to see him. He's senile."

"I see. That must have been very distressing for you."

"In a way. But he didn't seem unhappy. . . . In a way it was for the best, because I couldn't have coped with any big emotional scene, and at his age nor could he, even if his mind had been stronger. What I've always loved have been his books. I've been proud to be the daughter of a great novelist."

"I remember a little about the affair. Was this another case of your mother sailing into a love affair and falling flat on her face?"

"Oh yes!" Cordelia shot him a brief, relishing smile. "I

was going to use it to open my memoir of her. That was
quite different from the Louis business. With Ben it was
pure shortsighted self-aggrandizement. Here was this great
novelist, tired of writing fiction, maybe written out or just
bored with life, whom she thought she could galvanize into
writing a great play for her. Remember, she was not well
known then, merely promising. He was going to write a
great play, with of course a great part for her."

"And it didn't work out like that?"

"Not at all. What she got out of it was me, and *The
Vixen.*"

"That's a novel, isn't it?"

"Yes, with her as the central character—a ruthless, preda-
tory, humorless monster. Though ultimately the character is
funny, or funny, *too,* because of her total lack of self-knowledge and because she is so young. One thinks of monsters of
that sort as mature or old, but here was a full-fledged horror
still in her early twenties. Miriam, the Myra figure in the
book, lives in a sort of self-made bubble. She can't have real
relationships because she hasn't the slightest understanding
of how other people think or feel."

"He wrote the book just after the relationship ended, did
he? Wasn't that rather unnecessarily cruel?"

"I suppose so. I know my father wasn't perfect. Roderick
saw them together, and he had the impression that Ben was
studying Myra, like some sort of specimen, intending all
along to use her. I realize that's not nice. . . . But Myra
did that all the time, too, you know. She created a lot of
roles purely from the outside—gestures, walks, speech man-
nerisms. She used to hit on people similar to the character
she was to play and milk them for all they were worth."

Meredith was amused by her apparent readiness to admit
her father's faults, coupled with the more pressing urge to
emphasize that her mother was much worse.

"So your mother had good reason to hate your father?"

"Oh, very good reason."

"And perhaps your father to hate your mother?"

"Do you think so? I've found no evidence that he did.

Essentially he won. He played with her for some months, then got a book out of her."

"She certainly threw mud at him in the gutter press."

Cordelia shrugged. "Ben was above being harmed by the gutter press. I've read his letters. I don't have the impression he minded."

"I'm just looking for possible motives."

"If you knew—" Cordelia stopped. "If you knew how feeble he is, and how feebleminded, you wouldn't even bother to consider a motive for him."

Meredith nodded. "Maybe not. What was it your mother said about him that started the fighting?"

"Do I have to say?"

"I think so."

Cordelia looked down at the table, then said slowly: "She said . . . she said he quite likely wasn't my father. She said that she'd had it off with a Cameron Highlander on the train coming down, the weekend I was conceived."

"I see." Meredith did see the hurting accuracy of the hit. This girl had cherished the idea of her father more than anything in the world. "That must really have upset you."

"It seemed like she wanted to take my father away from me. Of course I realized later, when I was walking it off, that it was just Myra being Myra."

"What do you mean?"

"It was a very typical tactic. She knew I thought she was a lousy mother, she knew I worshiped my father, *ergo* she had to think of the most effective way of robbing me of him. Knowing her, the incident with the Cameron Highlander did occur at some time. She just remembered it, switched it in time, and used it to stick the knife in me."

"You're probably right. Tell me, how did the—the interview between you and your mother end?"

"Well, as you know, I threw myself on her, at her throat, and she was grabbing at my arms, trying to get me away, and we fell to the floor—" She stopped.

"Yes?"

"I suppose I just lost the urge, ran out of steam. Or suddenly saw how sordid and ridiculous it all was. I simply let go, got up, and she scrambled up, too. We looked at each other, and I said . . . something. What was it? Oh, yes, I said: 'You do have a great gift of bringing out the worst in everyone, Mother.' Then I went to the door and said: 'I hope I never have to see you again.' And then I left."

"What was your mother doing?"

"Just standing there, red and blotchy, *very* unattractive, looking at me with rage."

"And you didn't go back?"

"No. I got my wish. I never saw her again."

11

The next morning was a terrible time for Roderick and Caroline, the more so because nothing was happening that involved them. After breakfast they rang the police station at Cottingham and were told that Chief Inspector Meredith had talked to Cordelia the night before and that she was being held there for further talks, once the inspector had completed his work at the Red Lion, which was where he was at the moment. No, they couldn't say anything about when she would be released.

They felt completely helpless. The whole matter was in other hands, and God knew what the outcome would be. Roderick took Becky down the lawn to look in the tent, but he found that Pat had gone.

"He must have gone to the village early," he said to Caroline. "Probably to go to the Red Lion or to pick up any gossip that's going."

So there was nothing to do but wait. They played ball in the garden with Becky and tried not to let any of their worry get through to her.

Pat came back about half past ten. He was carrying a plastic bag laden with goods, for he had gone from shop to shop, intent on gleaning information from customers or shopkeepers but forced in all conscience to buy, as well.

"I rang the police from the call-box," he said, coming across the garden toward them. "They're not saying when they will let her go."

"We know. We rang them, too. We should have known they'd give nothing away. Did you find anything out?"

Pat slung his bag into the tent, and they all went and sat on the garden seat.

"The greengrocer had the most news. I'd forgotten he was actually there, in the Saloon Bar. I wasted time before that at the butcher's and the general store. You can imagine what it was like. Everyone went very quiet as soon as they saw me come in. They'd obviously decided already that Cordelia did it. Most of their information, when they unclammed, was punk: They said that Cordelia had been arrested, they said she'd shot her mother at the climax of a row, and so on. I hadn't got the full story then, so I couldn't contradict them with any confidence, but when I said I was sure that Myra was still alive when Cordelia left the Red Lion, they all got this obstinate look in their eyes, and I could tell they didn't believe me and would go on spreading their punk information."

"What about Mr. Allenby—the greengrocer?" asked Caroline.

"The whole of Maudsley's turning vegetarian for the day," said Pat dryly. "He's making a great thing of it. But presumably what he is giving out is accurate. When he says the row was long over when Myra was shot, people believe him, where they think I'm lying to shield Cordelia. He says Granville was in the bar all evening telling theatrical stories and getting quite a little group around him. Didn't even go out for a call of nature. The shot was heard about ten to ten. They all thought it was a car backfiring."

"Fair enough," said Roderick. "I can never distinguish the two."

"No. But then this woman came in and said she'd been in the loo and that the shot had been directly over her head. She was very insistent it had come from Myra's room, and rather reluctantly—because I don't think anyone really believed her—Granville went up to have a look. The whole bar was waiting at the door into the hotel section. They heard him open the door of his and Myra's room, find her dead, and rush down the stairs again. The landlord summoned the police at once."

They were all silent for a moment. They were all thinking of ways by which Granville Ashe could have done it. "It takes no time to shoot someone," "There are such things as silencers—" those were the sort of thoughts that were muddling around in their heads.

"I really am *not* going to start trying to find someone guilty," said Roderick firmly. "He seemed a perfectly pleasant young man, and I wouldn't have thought he'd have it in him, anyway."

He saw from the looks on the other two faces that they had all been thinking along the same lines.

"Anyway," said Pat, "if there's one thing that's clear about Myra, it is that she had plenty of enemies."

Meredith sat in the rather spare little hotel bedroom and talked to the woman who had insisted that what she had heard had been a shot.

She was, he decided, a perfect specimen of the English gentlewoman, a type that hardly seemed to have changed since his childhood. In spite of what must have been a quite horrendous evening and night, she was cool, rational, and polite. She wore a well-cut blouse and skirt, had pearls around her neck, and generally seemed as sensible and well-spoken a person as ever was a chairman of a Women's Institute branch or president of a local flower club. Meredith felt he had been meeting women like this all his life when he had been making public relations speeches to do-gooding organizations. If he had not been able to see her quiet but expensive luggage on the rack, her dressing gown hanging on a hook on the door, the little pile of books on her bedside table, he would have been able to make a very good guess at the sort of things she would buy, the sort of things she would wear, and the sort of things she would read.

She gave her name and address as Pamela Goodison, of 37, Fairview Road, London SW20. She said she was a widow.

"When my husband was alive, we always used to go abroad in summer. I know I shouldn't think of 'abroad' as being full of men waiting to rob or seduce single ladies of a certain age—and really I *don't*—but still I find I don't want to travel on the Continent on my own. So since my widowhood I generally go to favorite parts of Britain, staying a night here, two nights there, then driving on. It's pleasant and varied, and keeping on the move prevents one becoming the 'person on her own' whom everyone takes pity on and makes conversations with."

"Someone said your husband was an architect."

"Yes. That's partly the point. You see, we used to go around viewing houses together. Sometimes houses that Charles would decide to buy, restore, and redecorate, then sell at a profit. Sometimes houses he was investigating for clients. So over the years I have acquired a very good feel for the *shape* of a house. What is on each floor and how it all fits together."

"Let's go over exactly what happened last night. Now you . . . went to the toilet."

Mrs. Goodison smiled, but with a faint, gentlewomanly embarrassment.

"Yes. Not something one normally talks about in detail. It must have been about ten to ten, or a bit before."

"Which, er, cubicle were you in?"

"The middle one. There are three, and I was in the second along. It has a . . . well . . . a nasty piece of graffiti scrawled on the door. A male organ with a rude message underneath. I expect it's a sign of growing old, but women's loos would *never* have had that sort of thing in a respectable pub in my younger days. Is it a change for the better? I really can't persuade myself that it is. Anyway, that's where I was."

"And then the shot came?"

"That's right. I looked at my watch not long after, when

I'd absorbed the implications, and it said eight minutes to ten. I *knew,* you see, that it was a shot, and I knew it came from directly above me. There were no open windows anywhere in the ladies' loo, and I could *feel* the sound, the impact, from above me. Does that sound silly?"

"Not at all."

"So I sat there thinking: Whose room would that be? And of course everyone staying at the hotel had registered Dame Myra and noted which was her room. I'd seen her going in and out more than once. As soon as I got my 'architect's eye' working, I realized her room was directly above me."

"And you thought you ought to say something?"

Mrs. Goodison looked troubled.

"Yes. *Please* don't think I'm prejudging things or trying to put ideas into your head, but you see, earlier in the evening —Well, I'd better explain in detail. I was sitting reading in the bar for most of the evening. It had seemed a pleasant place, and it's nicer than shutting oneself up in one's room; one can have a drink, and there are people round one to look at now and again. I enjoy sizing people up, listening to them. But I don't actually want to *talk,* not if I've got a good book. Well, there was this silly woman—"

"Do you know her name?"

"I'm afraid not. And ignore that 'silly.' I barely spoke to the woman. I was merely reacting to the way she dressed. Anyway, she sat at my table before dinner, when there were very few seats left in the bar. She hadn't intruded, as I'd feared, but I'd observed her from behind my book, as I like to. She was very much taken up with Myra Mason and her family at a table nearby. Noticing everything that was to be noticed. Well, there was nothing very remarkable about that; practically everyone in the bar was conscious that there was a celebrity in our midst. Anyway, after dinner—no wait. I did notice during dinner that this woman went up to Dame Myra's table."

"And spoke to her?"

"Yes, spoke to all of them. Rather nervously, I suspected, as if she wasn't sure of her reception."

"And was it an amicable encounter?"

"I think so. . . . No sign of anything else that I saw. Though the woman, as I say, was standing tensely, fluttering her hands, and so on—jerky might be the best word. Well, after dinner, she was sitting at a table near mine. There were fewer in the bar by now, so she could have a table to herself. She still seemed rather jumpy. Then twice she got up and went into the hotel part of the building, and after the second time, I saw her talking to Dame Myra's husband and his group. When she came back to her seat, she leaned over to me at my table and said—do you want her exact words?"

"If you can remember them."

Pamela Goodison screwed up her eyes. "Let me see. 'It's really rather awful. There's a terrible row going on upstairs between Dame Myra and her daughter. And her husband won't do anything about it.' "

"What did you say?"

"Something soothing about it not being unknown for parents and children to quarrel. And she said: 'But this is *violent*. They are fighting. It's awful for me. Because in a way I'm connected with them.' Obviously I was supposed to ask how she was connected, but I knew that *that* would have spoiled the rest of my evening, so I made a few sympathetic clucking noises, said I was sure it would all blow over, and went back to my book."

"I see. And you remembered that conversation when you heard the shot."

"Yes. But there was no row while I was in the loo, and I'm *not* suggest—"

Meredith put up his hand.

"And I'm not suggestible, Mrs. Goodison. I don't jump to conclusions. Please give me credit for that. Anyway, this lady effectively made sure that the whole bar knew about the quarrel upstairs."

"That was certainly the effect. Whether it was the intention, I don't know. But if she was connected with the Masons by some *family* link, it certainly seems an odd way to behave."

"One more point, Mrs. Goodison. While you were . . . there in the toilets—"

"Yes? Oh, dear, this is the best-documented trip to the loo of my whole life."

"Did you hear anything else? Anyone running down the stairs? Any of the doors slamming? Things like that."

Mrs. Goodison wrinkled her forehead. "That's very difficult to say. A shot one remembers, but normal hotel noises one would hardly even register. And would one hear them in there? The stairs are well-carpeted . . . Wait. I was of course more conscious *after* the shot. While I was trying to work out which room it had been in. I *think* I heard the fire-escape door shut—I wouldn't swear to it, but I think so. But it's not something I could take my oath on in court—"

It all tallied precisely, as Inspector Meredith had known it would. Mrs. Goodison was a first-rate witness, the witness of any policeman's dreams. On the door of the central cubicle of the ladies' lavatories there was a crudely drawn penis with "THERE'S NOTHING WRONG WITH THE BRITISH BANGER" scrawled underneath. There were several other examples of similar wit here and there around the little cubicle, including lesbian and feminist wit: "NICE GIRLS DO IT TOGETHER" and "THERE'S NOTHING WRONG WITH MEN THAT CASTRATION DOESN'T CURE." It was all pretty much on a level with a men's lavatory, but Meredith was sure that Mrs. Goodison was right: Twenty or thirty years ago the door would have been bare.

Where she had been sitting was directly under Myra Mason's room—directly under the door of it, where the report would have been loudest. Here there would be the least likelihood of confusing it with a backfiring car outside.

It was as he was emerging (with that slightly furtive air that was inevitable) from the ladies' lavatories that Meredith was stopped.

"Excuse me. You are the policeman on the Myra Mason case, aren't you?"

It was a whole family, one that had clearly waited for him

at the bottom of the stairs. Both father and mother were fresh faced, healthy types, sensibly dressed for outdoors, with modest English tans. They had two girls and a little boy dressed in down-to-earth, dirtiable clothes.

Meredith nodded.

"You see we heard about the shooting, inevitably, when we got back last night, and now we've heard all the people talking in the village." The father stopped.

"We're worried, you see," the wife took up, "because people say the daughter has been arrested."

"People say all sorts of things," said Meredith. "That's not in fact the case."

"Oh, I *am* glad. We had to come and see you, though, because in fact we saw her."

"Saw Cordelia Mason? Where?"

"Down on the beach. We were all down there. We had a late swim, and we'd been collecting shells."

"When did you see her?"

"That's easy. When the light failed. We were about to start up the cliff path. We let the children stay up late on holiday, you see, but this was really late. Say half past nine."

"We'd seen her earlier in the bar," said the husband. "When they all four were sitting there, before dinner. There's no question that it was her. She's a big girl, and one noticed her. She was walking on the beach—looking very thoughtful, maybe unhappy. She started up the cliff path after us."

"How long after you?"

"Two or three minutes. We saw her beneath us."

"And when did you get back here?"

"Just before ten. It was absolute bedlam in here."

"And there is only the one path up?"

"Just the one. And she didn't pass us on the way. We're really glad she is not under arrest." He looked at his wife, both of them glad they'd done their duty. "If anybody's in the clear, she is."

12

The Red Lion at Maudsley had been modernized ten years before Myra's death there, but it had not been made luxurious. It was not that sort of hotel. Its clientele in the spring and summer months were mainly walkers, or middle-class couples in cars, many of them elderly. There were also families who wanted the sea without all the horrors of the British sea*side*. They had money to spend but not to chuck around. Those who had money to chuck around—usually company money, other people's money—went to classier establishments in large towns.

Myra Mason's room—or, rather, the Ashes' room—had a bathroom annex, but so did most of the other rooms, and its superiority to them consisted mainly in its being slightly larger and having a little extra furniture: two armchairs instead of one, an occasional table on which room-service meals could be set out, and an elaborate dressing table that Myra had made good use of. It was still fairly basic: The wallpaper seemed to have been chosen at random, and the picture over the bed was any old Spanish street corner in any old Spanish town. Any individuality the room had had been given it by Myra herself.

The body of Myra was no longer there. It had lain back against the pillow on the left-hand side of the bed, with a hole through the temple. The bullet had gone through the bedhead and into the wall behind. From its position it was clear that Myra had been lying on her back—thinking? meditating revenge on her daughter?—had struggled upward when her murderer had come into the room, and had sunk back when she had been shot. There had been on her face an expression that Meredith found difficult to define: surprise, bewilderment—neither word quite summed it up. Puzzlement perhaps came nearest. Not so much "Why are you shooting me?" (as it might be, if, say, her new husband had appeared in the doorway with a gun in his hand) as "Who are you?" or "What are *you* doing *here*?" But expressions on dead faces, Meredith knew, could be misleading or worse; trick reactions of muscles could render them farcically inappropriate comments on the actual circumstances of death.

Yet the expression remained with him: Who are you? What on earth is happening? Is this a joke?

The body had gone, and the gun had gone. It had been dropped on the carpeted floor not far from the door. He would be getting a report on that, too, before long. Guns had not loomed very large in Meredith's criminal investigations hitherto; by no means as large as if he had been an American policeman or one active in one of the larger British cities. Two questions occurred to him: The murderer had left the gun rather than taken it with him. Less potentially incriminating that way, presumably. But what did that tell him about the murderer?

And then there was the question of a silencer.

This was a question that had never come up in Meredith's experience, but it intrigued him. He knew enough about them to know that Granville Ashe, on going up to the room he had shared with his wife, could not have shot her with a revolver that had a silencer attached, removed the silencer, then rushed downstairs. The time factor, so far as he had grasped it from the testimony of all the people waiting at the door downstairs, rendered this an impossible supposition. But was there some other possibility? That Dame Myra had been shot *earlier* with a silencer and the shot Mrs. Goodison heard had been a mere blind, to establish an alibi, maybe? No—that wouldn't work. Someone had to be in the room, making the noise.

Meredith shrugged off the temptation to go up blind alleys and turned his attention to what this drab, characterless hotel bedroom actually told him.

The wardrobe was less full than he might have imagined, but then, he had no evidence that Myra had intended to stay beyond a few days. A very smart woolen suit, a severely cut skirt, and four really beautiful dresses—simply, shapely, of subtle, not readily definable colors. A lady who was conscious of her appearance, but cleverly rather than ostentatiously so. Expensive clothes, nevertheless. Much more so than her husband's, which took up as much space in the wardrobe and which were never more than goodish. Granville was better, though, at leisure wear—pleasant, sporty, light clothes, suitable for summer days near the sea. Nothing Myra had could remotely have been described as informal. Meredith guessed that she had never had a lot of time for leisure.

This was confirmed by some of the personal things around the room. Whereas Mrs. Goodison had brought books with her, Myra had brought scripts. There were no books at all, at least not ones for leisure reading. Instead, there was one of this year's new plays by Alan Ayckbourn, Shaw's *Getting Married,* a new translation of a Strindberg, an Edward Bond script, and *The Cherry Orchard.* It was the Ayckbourn or the Strindberg that she had been reading before she died— both of them were facedown on her bedside table. Meredith glanced at them. The Strindberg was *The Father.* A suitable play for a woman in a rage? he wondered. The Ayckbourn was apparently a middle-class comedy with a strong central role for a middle-aged woman. All the plays were heavily marked in red—words underlined in the main woman's part, little lines suggestive of possible intonations, pauses marked in. Myra, as everyone agreed, was a professional.

There was no great quantity of jewelry. Why should there be for a few days in the country? Beside the bed was a

necklace—presumably one that Myra had been wearing earlier in the evening, taken off when she had put on her nightdress and carelessly left there rather than put in the little
leather-covered box that held the rest of her things. These
consisted of five other pieces: a necklace of pearls, two
brooches, and two rings. Few but good seemed to be the
motto here, as with the clothes. One brooch in particular, a
Victorian setting of a diamond—large, sparkling, decidedly
ostentatious—surrounded by sapphires, seemed a very valuable piece indeed, unless Meredith's eyes were playing him
false. Dame Myra, he remembered, had had many admirers
—many *lovers,* he corrected himself, scorning euphemism—
and her jewelry was probably in the main gifts from them.
No doubt she had earned plenty of money herself over the
years, but he guessed that for a woman like her jewelry
would be something she would expect to have bestowed on
her.

The main sign of lavishness, of conspicuous consumption,
was on the dressing table. Here there were jars and bottles,
sprays and compacts, drops and syringes in great abun-
dance. That the products were expensive was evidenced by
the containers, which all looked as if they had been dreamed
up by Italian designers and executed in exclusive glass-blow-
ing establishments in Venice. He wondered what she had
done with them when they were empty; they were hardly the
sort of object one merely threw into the garbage bin. Studying the bottles, Meredith found a preponderance of skin
foods and moisturizers, with only a modest supply of lip-
stick or mascara. The important thing was the well-being of
the product rather than the painting of it. It occurred to
Meredith that Myra *ought* to have been a woman of great
good sense. Her care of herself, her presentation of herself,
were based on admirable criteria. No doubt it was when
other people intruded into her world that her judgment deserted her.

And then there was her notepad. This Meredith had observed on his first visit to the room, in the first minutes of
the police operation. It was a memo pad such as one could

obtain in any stationer's—square white paper with a design
of flowers printed on the sides. He guessed all the old sheets
had been torn off before it had been packed, for all the notes
on the top three sheets that had been used seemed to relate
to things that had come up since she came to the Red Lion.

On the top sheet was "Call from Harley re Mrs. Wilcox.
Ring from Pelstock." On the second sheet was "New tie for
G." and "Cordelia 6:15." Meredith went over to the wardrobe and looked at Granville's ties. Some were perhaps a
shade flamboyant, a bit airy. One, a stripe in blue and deep
purple, looked decidedly more expensive than the rest.
Granville, then, rated a new tie. Would he have had to stay
married longer to have rated a new suit?

The Cordelia reference was surely simple. It was the time
she and Pat were to come to the Red Lion on the murder
night. But the third sheet was puzzling. It read: "Woman for
Ayckbourn. TV. Oaken Heart? The Blush?"

It was the last note on the pad. Had it been written
shortly before she was killed?

When he got back to the police station at Cottingham, Meredith rang the Cotterels. He told them he was going to have
a brief chat with Cordelia but that after that he would hold
her no longer. Would they come and get her, or should he
send her back to the Rectory in a police car? They would
come and get her. Oh, and would they and Miss Mason's
boyfriend hold themselves in readiness for questioning tomorrow? He had a myriad things to do for the rest of the
day, including questioning the husband, but earlyish tomorrow? . . . That was kind of them.

When Cordelia was brought into the interview room by
Sergeant Flood, she assured him she'd slept well and late,
had been brought an excellent breakfast, and had generally
been well looked after. She had also been brought the papers, she said, but there had naturally been little that was
substantial about the death of her mother, so she was still in
the dark about many aspects of her killing.

"So are we," said Meredith. "But the important thing I

should tell you at once is that you were seen on the beach around the time the murder apparently took place. By a family that was down there, one that was staying at the hotel, and had seen you earlier. It seems a watertight alibi. We would like you to stay in this area for the next few days, if you would, but beyond that you're free to go."

Cordelia nodded. There was no expression of joy or relief. Meredith permitted himself to say: "You take it very coolly."

"There was always too much emotion in our house," Cordelia said with a sad smile. "I've tried to cultivate coolness —not always successfully."

"You've certainly not pretended to grief over your mother."

"No. There is none. A sort of sadness, maybe. But when you've said to yourself so often, 'I'd like to kill her,' it's almost comforting to find that you haven't."

Meredith found her gaucheness rather appealing.

"I've been looking round your mother's room. There seems to be some rather good jewelry there."

"Oh, yes. Mother had some wonderful pieces. She always chose her gifts herself. She had a great deal at home, but she wouldn't carry much around with her."

"There was a splendid diamond-and-sapphire brooch."

"That was given her by my father, by Ben Cotterel, shortly before I was born. Yes, it's beautiful. How typical of Myra to bring it when she came here."

"The fact that it's still in her room seems to prove that robbery was not the motive for the murder."

"I suppose so. I never thought it was."

"You thought it must be something in her relationships or in her earlier life?"

"That seemed the most obvious possibility, if you knew Myra and her genius for making enemies."

"I was thinking about the men in her life. You're the obvious one to know most about that. Do you think you could make a list of them for me?"

Cordelia laughed, a frank, almost happy laugh. "You

know not what you ask. The ones I know about would fill two foolscap pages, and there were many I didn't."

"Could you try, anyway? Perhaps you could indicate whether they were short-term relationships or longer ones, whether they lived together, and so on. And perhaps you could indicate whether the men were married at the time of the affair."

"I can try. I wouldn't always know if they were married or not, though often Myra told me; it gave the affair added spice, added éclat. She knew I'd feel sorry for the wives—though really I felt sorriest for the men."

"So you'll give it a try for me?"

"Yes, I will. But remember, I really only know about the ones from the time I got to the age of noticing. About the earlier ones I know nothing at all."

"Except your father," said Inspector Meredith.

"Right. Except my father. And the soldier from the Cameron Highlands," said Cordelia with a nervous laugh.

"I expect your relatives will be waiting to take you back to the Rectory," said Meredith as he shepherded her from the interview room. "You are of course entirely free now, but I do have your word you will stay in this area for the moment, don't I?"

"Certainly."

"By the way, there was a note on your mother's pad: 'Call from Harley re Mrs. Wilcox.' Does that mean anything to you?"

"Harley is—was—Myra's agent," said Cordelia promptly. "Harley Clarkson. An address in Soho—Dean Street, I think. I don't know a Mrs. Wilcox. But could it be a part? There's a Mrs. Wilcox in *Howards End*. There's a bit of an E. M. Forster boom on at the moment. It could be a television adaptation or a film. It's a terrible book, but Mrs. Wilcox would be a good part. Moneyed but saintly. *Not* one of the parts that Myra would look inward for!"

"I see. There was another note. Just two names, or

phrases, 'Oaken Heart' and 'The Blush.' Do they mean anything to you?"

Cordelia frowned.

"I don't think so. Though 'Oaken Heart' rings a very vague bell. Could they be other possible parts, offered by Harley Clarkson? Myra was probably looking round for what to do after *John Gabriel Borkman*."

"Possibly. The two things were separated on the name pad. There could have been another call from the agent, I suppose. I'd better contact him and find out. . . . Ah, here are your relatives, and your boyfriend."

Oddly enough, Cordelia—who had been open to the point of ingenuousness with him and quite relaxed—became awkward when faced with Roderick and Caroline. However, she thanked them for coming to fetch her, then embraced Pat and started into a good old confab with him. Meredith noted these things, remembered his feeling of a slight tension the night before, then passed on to other work on the case. There was enough of that, in all conscience.

The Cotterels said they had the car out the back, in the station yard. They'd been allowed in there to avoid reporters and photographers. The story had broken on Fleet Street (or the various unappetizing locations replacing it) and was predictably about to become the week's sensation, replacing sexually abused children and a hot-air balloon trip across the Atlantic. Fleet Street liked variety. They got themselves into the car without incident, but they had to drive past the front of the station, and here the massed newshounds recognized Cordelia. The clicks of their cameras sounded like a demented abacus.

In the car on the way home Cordelia chatted away, mostly to Pat. Caroline asked whether she had been well treated, and Cordelia waxed quite enthusiastic about Meredith.

"Really very sweet and gentle. The nice kind of Welshman, not the rugby-football hearty type. I should think he's a dogged soul who will worry away at the case until it's eventually solved. . . . If you care about that." She turned back to Pat. "Do you know, I realized in that police station that I don't really care who killed Mother. I don't hope he gets away with it, I don't hope he gets caught, I just don't care. I wonder if there's something wrong with me."

Roderick and Caroline left them to it. It was their liberation, after all, their relief. But Caroline did say to Cordelia: "I must say I admire you. You took it all so coolly. Almost nonchalantly. I should have been terrified, however innocent."

"Somehow I never thought I was going to be accused of it," said Cordelia reflectively. "Silly, really, when you think how many people have been wrongly convicted of murder. Evans, and probably the Carl Bridgewater people, and the pub bombers. And I suppose I took it coolly because I knew that one phase of my life was over. Such a relief. No more need to struggle against her or gain petty revenges on her for the way she treated me years and years ago. I can be me instead of Myra's child."

Outside the Rectory gates there was another little knot of reporters aiming their lethal weapons at Cordelia in the backseat.

"I shall never get used to it," said Caroline.

"I've had it all my life," said Cordelia. "In a mild sort of way."

Roderick pulled the car up just outside the front door, and they got out onto the gravel driveway. Pat had bought a chilled bottle of champagne at the Maudsley off-license, and he marched off down to the tent to open it. Cordelia, though, lingered, suddenly awkward again.

"I wanted to say I'm sorry," she said, her hands working feverishly. "For what I said last night. You've got to remember I'm Myra's child: I've never learned to behave."

"That's quite—"

"And I see why you did it. It was for Becky, wasn't it? So the royalties would continue for her lifetime, to assure her future after you're both dead. I should have thought of that." As Roderick opened his mouth to comment, Cordelia brushed him aside with a gesture. "Sorry. I really am sorry. I won't mention it again. Nobody knows. Even Pat doesn't know."

And she turned from them and ran down to the tent.

13

"Why did you marry her?"

Chief Inspector Meredith had not intended to ask the question, at least not bluntly in that way. He had intended to touch on it obliquely, hope to capture straws in the wind. For there was no guarantee that the answer would be the truth or that the man would even be self-aware enough to formulate an answer. Why people marry whom they do is often enough a mystery to themselves as well as to their friends.

Yet Granville Ashe sat there in the interview room, open, appealing, frank in a fairly lightweight kind of way, and somehow the question had popped out. It was a case of the human factor intervening, as, in Meredith's experience, it so often did in the course of an interview.

Granville was wearing his only suit, or the only one he had brought with him; it was darkish, but far from mourning, and he also had on the blue-and-purple-striped tie. He was a little sad in mien—bewildered, shocked still, but making no claims to overwhelming grief. At Meredith's question he scratched his ear.

"It wasn't a whirlwind affair, you know. I'd known her a while back—twelve years ago, when I was a *very* young actor. I'd got on well with her then."

"That hardly seems to have been the general experience. What were the qualities needed to get on with her?"

Granville grinned. "You had to be self-effacing, not really competitive—which I'm *not,* as you can see from the progress of my career. You had to be basically a peacemaker, a douser of fires. . . ."

"This doesn't seem to have been the type that Dame Myra went for in the past."

"Not as *lovers.* I thought we were talking about getting on with her. No, in her lovers she wanted excitement, constant electricity, and the sort of sexual charge and inventiveness I lay no claims to. But her emotional life had been a series of disasters, and even someone as little self-critical as Myra had to realize that eventually. A small degree of self-knowledge may have come to her at last. I think in a way I represented the peace of the double bed after the hurly-burly of the chaise longue."

"But that doesn't answer my question," insisted Meredith, "of why *you* married *her.*"

"No." Granville paused thoughtfully. "I thought I could get on with her—and I *did,* in the short time we were married. I thought she was a great actress, much in demand, and therefore a person with influence. If I had to cling to her coattails to get West End parts, then cling to them I would. She was also not rich, but comfortably off—settled bourgeois prosperity after an eternity of theatrical digs. That, putting it at its lowest, is why I married her. But I also admired her exceedingly. I was astonished when the question came up but also immensely exhilarated."

"She brought the question up?"

"Oh, of course. I wouldn't have *dared.* . . ."

"I imagine you had some doubts about accepting, as well?"

"Oh, some, naturally. I represented them as being about the difference in our ages, but that wasn't it at all. There was her temper, her all-absorbing egotism, her demand for absolute loyalty. . . . She has this dresser, you know—the old-fashioned type of theatrical dresser: rod of iron and heart of gold and totally, but totally, loyal to Myra. I'm afraid Myra thought the whole world should be a permanent theatrical dresser. *Her* theatrical dresser."

"And did the daughter enter your calculations about whether to marry her or not?"

"Cordelia? No. Why should she? The subject never came up before the marriage. I knew she would now be grown up, and I assumed she'd married, or got a job, and they'd drifted apart. It seemed eminently likely."

"You'd known Cordelia before?"

"I'd met her. During our earlier . . . liaison. She was a teenager then. One had to feel sorry for her."

"Why?"

"She was looking for love and never finding it. Myra was the last of the ice-cold mommas, you know. Or at least, she was any and everything. Sometimes there would be demonstrations of affection that weren't entirely aimed at the press or public. It was a performance, but a private one. At other times—and mostly—there'd be rows, nagging, or simple neglect. She would like to have been able to forget Cordelia entirely. She had been a mistake, a miscalculation. I have the idea that by writing this book, Cordelia was serving final notice on Myra that she would never be able to forget her."

"Ah, yes," said Meredith, settling back in his seat. "Let's come to the book, and that last evening. What did your wife hope to gain from the meeting with Cordelia?"

"The suppression of the book. No question of that. She wanted me to act as go-between and peacemaker, and I was certainly willing to be that, but I knew they had to have a face-to-face first. Myra had been incredibly worked up since she heard about the book—she'd had whispers of it first from her dresser. Then, not long after we were married, we were in the pub in Pelstock, and she heard that Cordelia had come here to Maudsley. Then it began to get through to her what sort of a book this was going to be. She was so angry that I knew she had to boil over first, before she could begin to simmer down. So I was saving my energies till after the

slanging match. Once that was out of the way, I was sure
something could be worked out."

"What actually happened last night?"

"Well, the first part of the evening went perfectly well.
Not warm or happy or spontaneous, but all right. Tense,
though. One or two little awkwardnesses, as when Myra
pretended to be worried that Pat couldn't support them both
on a teacher's salary. She implied they were one degree up
from itinerant tinkers, which, even in this day and age, is
something of an exaggeration. It was easy enough to smooth
that over."

"You were interrupted during the early part of the evening, weren't you?"

"Interrupted? Oh, you mean . . . Wait—we were interrupted *twice*. The first was the commodore—Crutchley, or
some such name—with whom I finished the evening. Tremendous 'simple-old-sea-dog' act and a hard little wife with
a tremendous bust. Anyway, that was a straightforward case
of intrusion. Anyone in the theater, particularly anyone
prominent in the theater, knows about that kind of thing
and how to deal with it."

"And the other?"

"Yes. That was a woman who was—let's get this right—
Benedict Cotterel's daughter and therefore in a sense Cordelia's half sister. Something she rather insisted upon. I found
this intrusion very odd, unaccountable. I mean, it's not a
relationship one would push in the circumstances, is it? And
particularly not with someone as formidable as Myra
around. But she came over at dinner, made known who she
was, and tried to press friendship and hospitality on Cordelia, whom apparently she'd already met. It was all rather
embarrassing. Myra, predictably, made her feelings known."

"How?"

"As the woman was going back to her own table, Myra
said in a loud voice that Ben had told her that one of his
children was a prig, the other a fool."

"I see," said Meredith. "Interesting. Go on with your evening."

"Well, at the end of the meal Myra announced that she and Cordelia had something to discuss, and she marched her upstairs. The boy—Pat—came with me into the bar, and we got drinks. We sat near the simple sailor man and his wife, and gradually we got talking. They knew nothing about the theater, of course, but thought it was glamorous to hear behind-the-scenes anecdotes. That's par for the course with the general public. But then this woman came back."

"Cotterel's daughter?"

"Yes. Going on about Myra and Cordelia rowing upstairs. Well, that was absolutely what I'd been expecting—quite inevitable, and probably healthy—so I certainly wasn't going to intervene. More than my life was worth, let alone my marriage. I persuaded Pat to take the same line, and she had to slope off. She was just mischief making, anyway, or sensation seeking. So we went back to theatrical anecdotes, and a little crowd collected around. Pat left after one drink, but I was there until—until we heard the shot."

"You didn't leave at all—to go to the toilets or anything?"

"No. I realize that could be important, but the crowd around me will back me up on that."

"And the Critchleys?"

Granville's forehead creased.

"Oh, dear. Is that important? I *think* he did, but I simply can't remember whether she did or not."

"Go on."

"Well, that's it, really. I went on delving into my repertoire of theatrical disaster stories until we heard the shot. We decided it was a car backfiring, and I went on talking until this very nice, concerned lady came along and said she was sure the shot had come from our bedroom. It all became nightmarish after that. I tried to pooh-pooh the idea, but she was very insistent, and still more people collected around the table, scenting some kind of sensation or disaster—maybe even hoping for one. No—I'm being unfair to most of them, I expect, but I remember being conscious of one face, Ben Cotterel's daughter, there in the crowd, and *avid*—do you know what I mean?"

"I do. Hoping for something terrible."

"Yes. Like the people in New York who shout 'jump' to suicides."

"Had she been in the bar all evening since she told you about the row?"

"I really hadn't noticed. Too taken up with my own performance. And in fact I certainly tried to put her out of my mind. She had seemed to me an eminently dislikable woman."

"So eventually you felt you had to go up."

"Yes. If only to damp down all this sensational expectation that had built up. So I went into the hotel section, and everyone followed me to the door. I went upstairs, got to the landing, and opened the door—"

"How?"

"It wasn't locked, though of course I had a key, anyhow. It was pretty dark in there. I whispered 'Myra,' but there was no reply, and so I turned on the light. For a split second I thought she was asleep. . . . Then I saw the hole. It was quite awful, terrible. Then I ran downstairs."

Meredith nodded. "Right. Well, that all ties in pretty well with what other people have told me. I must just ask this, Mr. Ashe: I suppose you benefit financially from Dame Myra's death?"

Granville Ashe grimaced. "I suppose so. I'm going to have to talk to Cordelia about this, because I don't want injustice to be done. But one thing I haven't told you—because it sounds awfully fanciful, I suppose—is that, somehow, I almost feel as if one of the reasons Myra married me was precisely to *have* someone to leave everything to other than Cordelia. Does that sound daft?"

"Not necessarily. Why do you think that?"

"Just the way she announced it a few days after we were married. She had been in to see her solicitor in Sudbury. The way she said she'd made a new will was sort of triumphant: 'That'll show her'—that kind of tone. They'd been on bad terms, or nonexistent terms, since Cordelia had moved in with Pat. She'd heard those whispers about the book. Apart from Cordelia, Myra had no one to leave whatever she had to, and that in itself must have been rather a desolating thought, particularly at her age. Marrying me was Myra's revenge. If I'm right, it's very unjust, and I'm going to have to go and see Cordelia about it. Something's going to have to be arranged."

In fact, Granville drove out to see Cordelia that evening. He had spoken to Myra's solicitor on the phone in the late afternoon, and in their guarded way they had completely understood each other on the subject of the will. Granville had said that it seemed to him damned unfair on the girl, who'd had a pretty raw deal most of her life. The lawyer had said that the sentiment did him credit, but he had urged caution. (When did lawyers urge anything else?) He said that—though Cordelia could always contest it—the will was perfectly legal, it clearly represented Dame Myra's actual wishes, and it was quite usual for the spouse to be the sole beneficiary, even when there were children. The fact that Myra and Granville Ashe had been married a comparatively short time (what would he have considered a short time? Granville wondered) was neither here nor there. If he felt that there was injustice involved, he could himself make a will in Cordelia's favor.

"I am not that much older than Cordelia," said Granville dryly. "So I don't think that would fill the bill."

The result was that in the evening he drove Myra Mason's two-year-old Mercedes in the direction of the Rectory. It was by no means the first time he had driven it, but now, being alone and virtually its owner, the drive gave him a distinct feeling of power.

Caroline and Roderick were surprised to see him, but they all got through the business of proffering and receiving condolences gracefully. The Cotterels were impressed by Granville's avoidance of any histrionic extremes of grief. They found him quietly dignified. They settled him into an armchair, well away from Becky and the television, and pressed whiskey on him.

"My main reaction is one of surprise," Granville said as he took the glass.

"Surprise? But presumably—" Caroline caught herself up just as she was going to say something tactless. "I mean, it's possible Dame Myra had a lot of enemies in the theater, isn't it?" she emended. "It's that sort of profession, surely."

"Oh, certainly. But this is *not* the way theatrical feuds usually end. Nor family feuds, either. Frankly, I never for one moment thought that Cordelia did it, and I gather she now has the firmest of alibis."

"We never believed she did it, either. Though obviously she and her mother . . . didn't get along."

"And they never would. But it was the sort of relationship that led to stand-up rows, not to murder. By the way, Cordelia is the reason I'm here tonight. I wonder if I might have a word with her?"

"Surely. She'll be down in the tent. I'll get her," said Roderick, putting down his glass.

"We'll leave you alone when she comes," said Caroline. "I've got to put Becky to bed, anyway."

"No, please don't. It's nothing private. And I'd like to have you here. I find Cordelia rather an odd girl, and it would be nice to have some ordinary people around."

In the event, Cordelia brought along Pat, and they all went through the round of condolences again, this time rather awkwardly, since Cordelia and Pat's view of Myra was known to all present. Eventually they all subsided into chairs, clutching drinks.

"I had to come and see you, Cordelia," Granville Ashe began with touching formality, "because I spoke to your mother's solicitor this afternoon. He confirmed what I already suspected: that your mother had left everything to me."

Cordelia nodded.

"I say already suspected, because she never actually *told* me. What I imagined was that as soon as this business of the book blew over, Myra could be persuaded into making a will that was more equitable and, well, more fitting. No question of that now. Let me make this quite clear; as far as I am concerned, there's no way of seeing this will as anything other than unjust."

Cordelia frowned. "Unjust?"

"Of course it's unjust. You're her daughter, and I'm her husband of three weeks. So I wanted to see you straight away and make it clear that this will is *not* all right with me, and we're going to have to get together—us or our solicitors —and work something out."

"You mean you want to give me part of what you inherit from Myra?"

"Well . . . put bluntly, yes."

"But I don't want anything." She looked at Pat. "We don't want anything, do we?"

Pat shook his head, firmly and unhesitatingly.

"Look, Cordelia," said Granville persuasively, "you may feel like that now, and twenty-odd is the right age to be idealistic and otherworldly, but I assure you that you'd regret it in a few years' time if you refused. It's simply a question of justice. You're Myra's daughter, and you . . . well, you put up with a lot, we all know that. It's right you should have part of what she left."

Cordelia smiled. "It's very nice of you. Sort of quixotic. But I don't think the idea of justice comes into inheritance, do you? It's just a lottery. I mean, there's no *justice* in the eldest son getting most, but he generally does. Pat and I don't want any big sum of money suddenly falling on us. In fact, we'd rather not have too much."

"Much rather," said Pat decisively.

"And there's also the question of inclination. I wouldn't *want* to inherit anything from Myra. I hated her. Everyone here knows that. Even if she'd left me anything in her will, I'd refuse to accept it. It would be . . . distasteful. So please don't press me."

Granville turned to Roderick and Caroline. "You try to make her see sense."

"It's her decision," said Roderick slowly. "But I do think, Cordelia, that you might regret it later on."

"No. If I took anything, I'd regret it later on."

Granville looked at her helplessly. "Something personal. Some of her jewels. She has some quite beautiful things."

"Still less anything personal," said Cordelia. "Though you're quite right about the jewels. Some of them cost the earth. That necklace from Louis, for example. He moved heaven and earth to get it back when they split up, but he hadn't a hope."

"Would you accept it?"

"Good God! A memento of Louis! About the last thing I'd want," said Cordelia, shuddering. She stood up. "I'd much rather not talk about it anymore. Please get it into your head that I don't want anything and I won't accept anything." She paused at the door. "Oh, except for the books I made of her cuttings. I would like those."

"They weren't the sort of thing I was thinking of at all," said Granville.

14

Roderick and Caroline spent the morning of Wednesday doing odd jobs around the house. It was Mrs. Spriggs's morning for giving the downstairs "a good clean through," so they got down to doing little things that they'd said for years needed doing, though they'd never cared enough before actually to do them. In reality, they (and indeed Mrs. Spriggs, who was voraciously interested) were just waiting for Meredith.

They had discussed in bed the night before whether or not they should come clean with him, disburden themselves of the whole story, but they had decided there was now no greater reason than before to do so. That decision nevertheless hung over them like a black-edged cloud.

Cordelia did not come up to work on the Cotterel papers. That was natural enough, in the joy of her release from suspicion. But they did wonder whether she would in fact want to work on them again, whether her project had been laid to rest. Probably not, in view of her request to Granville of the night before. About eleven they saw her and Pat going off, towels over their shoulders, laughing happily.

"We told Pat that Meredith wanted him to be available today," said Roderick. "Do you think we should call them back?"

"It's their responsibility," said Caroline. "I don't think we should try to mother-hen them." Later she said: "Odd to think that three weeks ago, if someone had mentioned Cordelia Mason, we would have been hard put to think who was meant."

They lunched off bread and cheese. Mrs. Spriggs had to leave to feed her children from school, though clearly if she'd had her way, they would have gone hungry. When Meredith arrived, with Sergeant Flood, they were just settling Becky in front of the television for an Australian soap.

"Just come and stand around for a minute or two," said Caroline to the newcomers. "When she's used to your being here she'll watch the television quite quietly. . . . Who's that actor? I've seen him before."

"*Picnic at Hanging Rock,* I think," said Roderick. "Or maybe *The Chant of Jimmie Blacksmith.*"

"Poor man. I hope he made this soap *before* them and hasn't been reduced to it."

"Can't be much work in Australia for actors," said Meredith.

"Except the beer commercials," said Sergeant Flood.

Caroline nodded to them, and they all moved quietly away to the far end of the room.

"It's terrible just to sit her in front of the television," said Caroline, "but sometimes it's the only way. She likes seeing faces that she recognizes. Now she's got used to your being here, she won't worry us."

They settled down into a group of sofa and armchairs that Caroline had arranged specially. Flood got out his notebook and made some preliminary jottings.

"I'm sorry we're late," said Meredith. "I've had to talk to the Red Lion landlord and some of his guests who wanted to get away. Now—if we can just get the boring stuff out of the way. Such as what you were doing on Monday evening."

"Yes, of course," said Roderick. "We've thought about that. I was in and out of the study—my study, that is—in the earlier part of the evening. In and out because Becky was in here."

"I was gardening," said Caroline. "A little neglected patch, down at the end, near the new housing estate. I'm trying to grow wild flowers there, but they seem to be more trouble than ordinary garden flowers. Someone from the estate may well have seen me down there, and I was back and forwards to the toolshed. I came back in when the light began to fail, just after nine."

"And then we discovered we were out of milk," said Roderick. "Becky is absolutely miserable if she doesn't have her Ovaltine before bedtime, so I drove into the village, where there's a corner shop that stays open till ten in summer for the tourists and campers."

"I see. So you will have been there—when? Ten past nine? Later?"

"Quarter, twenty past, I should think."

"You went straight there and came straight back?"

"Yes. I can't have been gone more than twenty minutes."

"Right. And you stayed here, Mrs. Cotterel—naturally, with your daughter and the old gentleman to look after."

"Yes, I was here. We certainly don't leave Becky alone if we can help it, but Roderick's father can be left in the evening. He usually falls asleep around seven. He's so feeble that there's nothing he can really do, no harm he can come to."

"I see," said Meredith. Something I must check, he thought. He said: "Now, I'd better get this right: the old gentleman had an affair, many years ago, with Myra Mason."

"That's right. In the late fifties, early sixties. Cordelia is the result. It made quite a scandal at the time—at least the breakup of the affair did."

"The scandal being of Myra Mason's making?"

"Yes. She didn't go quietly. You might take the view there was no reason why she should," said Roderick.

"I have vague memories of the scandal. Would I be right in saying that the public was interested less because Myra Mason was a famous actress than because Benedict Cotterel was a famous novelist?"

"That's pretty much right. Myra was then still at the beginning of her career. Avid for any sort of publicity, if you put the worst construction on it. Just a bad manager of her private life, if you took the kindlier view. Anyway, there was one of those short-lived tabloid stinks, because my father was a very well known, slightly up-market novelist. If the truth were told, Fleet Street had probably known for years that he was something of a philanderer and had been waiting for dirt they could print without fear of a libel action. Myra handed it to them on a plate. The fact that she was a very beautiful woman didn't make the story any less attractive to them."

"I see. Will you pardon my ignorance if I ask what sort of a writer your father was . . . is?"

"Was, I'm afraid. No question of his ever writing again. I'm afraid we often think of him in the past tense. Well, it's not an easy question to answer. His first novel was published in 1927, you see, and his last nearly forty years later. The first was very lush, romantic, a young man's novel. In the thirties they became darker, more political—my father was very much part of the left-wing political scene, along with Orwell, Auden, and the rest. After the war they became sharper, more satirical—Ben always liked to say that comedy was much more difficult than serious stuff, and much more profound. There were a lot of travel books after the war, too, and even one about architecture. He always wrote wonderfully about places. About 1952 he stopped writing fiction except for some short stories, and *The Vixen*, his revenge on Myra."

"I always say that was unworthy of him," put in Caroline. "He may not have been a kind man, but he was usually a just one. *The Vixen* is very unjustly weighted—against Myra."

"Old men get selfish—self-absorbed," said Roderick. "If I had to sum up the fiction, I'd say they were generally about intelligent, aware people, in contemporary situations and dilemmas, with usually a strong love or sex interest."

"They sold well?"

"Very well. Penguin once published ten of his books simultaneously. He wasn't a mass-market writer, and he started to look a little out-of-date with the coming of the Angry Young Men, but he did have a large, literate following. We lived well."

"Ah, yes. You said he was a philanderer. What about his family life?"

"Oh, when I said we lived well, I meant the three of us left behind lived well—and he, too, on his own. All through our early childhood he was more away than at home. Early in the war he moved out for good."

"So there was no question of the affair with Myra Mason breaking up his marriage?"

"Good Lord, no," said Roderick, laughing. "It'd been broken up for years. Though there was never an actual divorce."

"And is your mother still alive?"

"She died in 1968," said Caroline. "I'm afraid you're barking up the wrong tree, Inspector."

"I have very few trees, Mrs. Cotterel, and I have to bark up each of them." Meredith settled back in his chair. "What I'm trying to get is a picture of Dame Myra's emotional life. Would I be right in thinking your father went into the affair in a rather detached, ironic way—an amusement for an aging man, a bit of not-too-serious dalliance."

"Yes . . . Yes, I think that would be fair," said Roderick.

"And that she took it much more seriously."

"Yes—though not, I think, if you mean that she was seriously in love with him. She was passionate, pushy, monomaniacal, but all for herself and her own career. That, anyhow, is how I read the situation."

"You met them together?"

"Yes. All the time it was as if Myra was battering her head against a rock. She could do nothing, because my father did not take her seriously and wasn't in love with her."

"I see . . . Would your sister have met them, too, at the time?"

"Isobel? Oh, no. No, she had very little contact with our father."

"Ah! Why was that, sir?"

"They just drifted apart, I suppose. That wasn't difficult, since we saw him so little during our childhood. She wanted to go and live with him in London soon after she left school, but he wasn't having any. I think that when that happened, she just shrugged him off. If he didn't want anything to do with her, she didn't want anything to do with him."

"And yet she comes to see him here?"

"Well—" Roderick and Caroline looked at each other. "Not really. She never bothers to go up and see him."

"She just comes to see you."

"Yes . . . Yes, she mainly comes to see us."

"I see. Well, I'll be talking to your sister—"

"Will you? I don't see what she can have to do with it."

"Nor do I, sir. Still, she overheard the quarrel between Dame Myra and her daughter. And in fact I'll be talking to everyone who was in the Red Lion that night—I or one of my men. Now, I'm going to make a request that I hope you don't find offensive. I wonder if I could see your father."

"Oh." Roderick looked at Caroline. "I don't see why not."

"No," said Caroline. "Would it be all right if only one of you came? He tends to find new faces confusing."

"Yes, that would be quite all right. I'll tell you why I ask. I took a copy of *The Vixen* home with me last night. Got it from the Cottingham library. I've only been able to skim through it, but it *is* pretty devastating."

"I know," said Caroline. "I find it a really distasteful book."

"So if one is looking for motive . . ."

They stood up, and Roderick said: "*The Vixen* is more motive for Myra to kill Ben, I should have thought. Ben in most ways won the victory. The picture of the young Myra in that book is quite unforgettable."

"I suppose so. But there is hatred there. . . ."

"Do you think so?" Roderick raised his eyebrows. "I dis-

agree. I don't think there was, on Ben's side. I believe he
. . . played with her but mainly delighted in revealing her
outrageous egotism. Anyway, this is a silly conversation. As
you'll see, the question of my father killing Myra simply
doesn't arise."

"I'm sure you're right, sir," said Meredith. "I'm just trying to clear the ground."

Sergeant Flood waited in the hall at the bottom of the
stairs, his notebook tucked into the back pocket of his trou-
sers. As the three of them proceeded quietly up the wide
stairway, an old voice made itself heard:

"And to my sister Dorothy . . . sister Dorothy . . . I
leave my . . . my yacht . . ."

"Oh, dear," said Caroline, darting on ahead. "He's at his
will-making again. . . . You've got visitors, Father."

By the time Meredith got to the door of the room, the
tape recorder had been switched off and the old man
plumped up in his bed. He looked to Meredith a very old
man indeed, and a bewildered one. Something about him
suggested that he had once been very active minded and
now could by no means comprehend that his mind was no
longer his servant.

"What?" he asked in his pale echo of a voice. "What,
Caroline? Who?"

Caroline bent over him. "It's Mr. Meredith, Father. A
visitor to see you."

"Who? Who?"

"Mr. Meredith," said Caroline brightly.

"I'm a policeman," said Meredith.

He sensed rather than saw the younger Cotterels stiffen.

"Policeman?" The voice gained a little more force but
rose in pitch. "Policeman?" He turned to Caroline, a dribble
of saliva running from the corner of his mouth. "What's a
policeman . . . ?"

The voice faded, as if he had a question in his mind that
he could not quite formulate. Caroline bent over again and
wiped his mouth. "Don't worry, Father. He's just here to
look at security."

"What? At what?"

"Security. You know, stopping burglars getting in and things like that."

The old head nodded twice from side to side, then closed its eyes. Caroline looked at Meredith, her eyebrows raised to ask if he needed to see any more. The policeman turned to go from the room.

"Well," he said at the bottom of the stairs, "I'm sure I won't need to trouble the old man again."

"You can talk to his doctor," said Roderick.

"I shall do that, of course. I'm sorry all this has had to be so unpleasant, but in the circumstances there's not much else I can do."

"We quite understand," said Caroline. "The fact that we find the notion of Ben nipping off to the Red Lion to kill one of his former girlfriends ludicrous and distressing doesn't mean you have to. You've never seen him before. But if you remember his age—eighty-six—and talk to his doctor, you'll see that it just isn't on."

"I really do see that already," said Meredith, letting Caroline open up the front door for him. "Now I just have to talk to Pat McLaughlin."

"Is that his name?" said Caroline. "I don't think I've ever heard it before. Anyway, they're back."

Standing on the gravel drive, they looked down toward the lawn, at the end of which, by their tent, Cordelia and Pat were lying on their stomachs, reading. Meredith turned, thanked Roderick and Caroline for being so helpful and understanding, then waited until they had gone inside and shut the front door.

He did not go at once down the garden. He stood there, Sergeant Flood waiting respectfully beside him (because he knew such moods in his superior), and let the impressions of the interview flow through his mind. At some time during the visit—before he had gone upstairs—something had clicked. There had been a . . . a reverberation, a message for him that something was not quite right, or maybe that something needed looking into. It hadn't been something falling into place but rather the reverse. . . . Some piece that had seemed to have a place but had suddenly become questionable. . . . Gone. He could not place it. But it would come back. They always did.

And then there had been the Cotterels, stiffening up, up there in the bedroom. When he had said he was a policeman. He was going to have to talk to Ben Cotterel's doctor. Unfortunately two people stiffening up was not evidence.

He squared his shoulders, grinned at Sergeant Flood, and started down the garden to talk to Pat.

15

The Cotterels heard from Pat next morning what had been said in his talk with the chief inspector. He and Cordelia were loading up the Volksie to set out for a day-long picnic on the Downs. When Caroline, with Becky, went out to them, they said they were going to take advantage of the fine weather. One might have guessed they were still in the middle of a perfectly ordinary holiday.

"How did it go with the police yesterday?" Caroline asked Pat.

He shrugged, his blue eyes, as so often, rather distant, as if this were some affair not really his.

"All right. Not much I could tell him, really. Granville and I went into the bar after dinner and drank beer. I didn't find him all that interesting, but a little knot of people began gathering round us, because of the Myra Mason connection, I suppose. He seemed rather to like having an audience, so I just slipped out. That was long before the shooting."

"And you came back here?"

"That's right."

"Drove?"

"Of course. Cordelia doesn't drive. I knew she'd be quite happy walking home."

Caroline realized she had begun to sound rather like a

police inquisitor herself, but she said: "Was the inspector happy with that?"

Pat shrugged again. "He had to be. It was the truth. In the nature of things you can't expect everyone to have an alibi."

"True," said Caroline. "We don't have watertight alibis ourselves. They say it's the ones with perfect alibis who are the most suspicious." She looked toward the Rectory gates, now largely unpicketed by reporters. "At least the press rabble seems to have moved on elsewhere."

"They've quartered themselves at the Red Lion," said Pat, getting into the car. "They've decided that's where the action is. We were down there last night, but they kept pestering us, so we came away."

There had been first a large, then a middle-sized, press contingent outside the Rectory gates since the news of the murder broke. Now there was just one man to snap Pat and Cordelia as they drove out through the gates and down the road toward Maudsley. The police had leaked the news that Dame Myra's daughter had been coming up from the beach at the time of the murder, and the press had concluded that they would have to get their leads elsewhere. The obvious place was the Red Lion, especially to a race of men and women for whom alcohol was a way of life.

Press coverage of the Myra Mason murder had been sensational—front page stuff every day since it broke. That was inevitable, given Myra's eminence and her private life. The press had a wad of material on her loves, her rivalries, her tantrums, including quite a lot of juicy items they had hitherto been chary of publishing. Death is a great unlocker of tongues, the libel laws being what they are. Every day, it seemed, was a field day. Former lovers were queuing up in Fleet Street to tell, or rather to sell, "their stories" to the various tabloid muckrakers. The titled lovers were offering themselves to the Sunday *Times*.

Coverage of the murder itself was, by comparison, vague. The papers knew the time of the shot and that it had been heard by "a woman" (Mrs. Goodison, doubtless conscious of the ludicrous aspects of her situation, had declined to talk to the press and had in fact moved on as soon as her usefulness to the police had ended), who had come to Dame Myra's husband and insisted that it be investigated. The place where she had been when she heard the shot was variously referred to as the toilet, the lavatory, the loo, the smallest room, and the little girls' room, depending on the class of the reporter or the nature of the newspaper he wrote for.

The latest new item of information in the papers that Roderick and Caroline flicked through at breakfast time had been the make of the gun—a Webley and Scott .38. This piece of information had been released by the police the day before. It was really the only piece of hard news. Otherwise, the papers filled in with contributions from the locals or from the tourists staying or drinking in the Red Lion: descriptions of how they had heard the shot in the bar, how shivers had gone down their spines, dread premonitions weighed them down, and so on, followed up by detailed accounts of how Granville Ashe had gone up to find the body. Isobel had yesterday given one reporter a detailed account of the row in Myra's bedroom that she had heard when she "happened" to go up twice to her own bedroom. Her shivers and her dread premonitions had apparently been even more pronounced than anyone else's. She was, she had told the reporter, psychic, or at any rate fey.

Isobel, in fact, was a surprise visitor that morning. More surprising still, she had walked from the Red Lion. She was, the Cotterels decided, "hyped up." When she walked into the sitting room, she forgot to do her usual performance of looking around appraisingly to see what outrages or acts of neglect they had perpetrated on "her" property. They decided she must have been unhealthily excited by all the sensation and publicity of the last few days, and in fact, as soon as she had lit up a cigarette, she drew from her bag a copy of the previous day's *Daily Star,* which had the interview with her in it.

"I knew you wouldn't have seen this, so I brought it

along," she announced. "You intellectuals always pretend to despise the popular press."

"I *do* despise the popular press," said Roderick. "But actually we have seen it. I drove into Maudsley yesterday to get all the papers."

"Feeling a bit guilty about it," Caroline's honesty forced her to admit.

"Still, an interest is natural," said Roderick. "And the popular papers sometimes get on to things the others have missed, particularly in cases like this. Of course, they've all raked up the business with Father again."

"Of course, an interest is natural," said Isobel, dismissing the business with Father with a wave of her hands—hands that in fact were today never still. She gazed at them greedily. "Wasn't it a *fabulous* interview?"

"Very . . . effective," said Roderick.

"Of course, all the reporters have been in and out of the Red Lion all the time, *buzzing* like bees round a honey pot," continued his sister with a kind of hectic complacency. "But I kept quiet and didn't say anything. Until this *awfully* nice young man approached me—terribly sweet, an awful flatterer"—her hands fluttered to her face, and the Cotterels had no difficulty imagining the extremes of flattery to which the young man had resorted—"so anyway, we had this long conversation in my room, and he said he'd *never* known a better interviewee than I was. Which bit did you like best? Did you like the bit where I said I thought it was a judgment on Myra for what she did to Father?"

Roderick had long ago decided that with his sister dishonesty was the best policy.

"Striking," he said. "A case of the mills of God grinding quite exceptionally slowly. I was surprised at your being so indignant on Father's behalf, though."

Isobel gave a gesture of contempt for the father angle. "Well, of course that was a sort of code for what I *really* meant. We had to talk a bit about Father to make quite clear who I *am*. What I really meant was the awful pain to *us*— to Mother—that the affair caused."

"Mother was upset by the publicity," Roderick admitted. "She was beyond being upset by Father's affairs by that stage."

"We were all terribly bruised by the publicity," asserted Isobel. Caroline could barely suppress a smile. Isobel had been married by the time the affair became public knowledge and (if her present conduct was anything to go by) had probably dined out on the publicity for weeks. "*Any*way, you've no idea of the excitement the interview has caused. Telephone calls from all *sorts* of people—friends, business associates of Cyril's, even my chiropodist. And Darrell has called to say he's coming to fetch me—which frankly he would *never* have done if he hadn't wanted to get in on all the excitement."

Darrell was Isobel's only son, whom Roderick had always found a particularly loathsome young man. Isobel's assessment of his character, he felt, was unusually accurate.

"Jolly good," he said.

"Of course, I can't go till I've talked to the chief inspector," said Isobel, her eyes sparkling unnaturally with anticipation. "That's this afternoon at half past three. I'm frightfully looking forward to it. I think he's an awfully attractive man, don't you?"

"And acute," said Caroline warningly.

"Oh, *naturally*. They'd put their best man on to the murder of Myra Mason, wouldn't they? I expect he'll be *very* interested in what I have to say."

In the event, Darrell Allick was already at the Red Lion when Roderick drove his sister back there. He recognized his back in the window of the Saloon Bar and turned the car straight round. Chief Inspector Meredith, that afternoon, was less lucky. Darrell drove his mother to the police station at Cottingham and insisted on escorting her in. His attentiveness to her was ostentatious but uncertain, as if he were unsure of how it was done. He was a fleshy, androgynous young man who seemed intent on bridging the gap between the sexes. Meredith, who happened to be talking to the duty sergeant, could hardly forbear a sharp intake of breath to indicate his distaste. When his mother was taken through to the interview room, Darrell sat in the outer office, double chinned and pop-eyed, reading stock market prices in the *Financial Times* and eating chocolate.

In the interview room Isobel Allick's performance was as nervous and gauche as it had been that morning at the Rectory. Perhaps she was unaware of the impression she made, perhaps she could do no other. It was difficult to imagine a manner less calculated to impress a policeman. One thing came forth very clearly: She was enjoying herself.

To calm her and to give himself time to assess her, Meredith took her through a recital of bare facts. Name: Isobel Allick. Date of birth: August 15, 1939. Place of residence: Dalberry House, Mitton, near Stroud. Husband's profession: Company director. Before long, however, Isobel had launched herself into a colorful account of The Quarrel.

"What struck me, you see, hearing the voices the first time I went up—I'm terribly sensitive to atmosphere, preternaturally, so my friends tell me—"

"Yes—I read your interview."

"Oh, *did* you? Well, as I said to the woman who sat next to me in the bar (she's been here when I've been here before, I think, though she wasn't very forthcoming)—as I said, what struck me was the *violence* in the voices. The sense of a coming storm. You could hear that Cordelia—poor Cordelia!—*hated* her mother, and in Dame Myra's voice there was sheer contempt." Isobel shuddered. "Contempt! Can you imagine it? For her own daughter! I can hardly bear to think about it. So, as I say, it was this premonition of *violence* that made me so afraid, *forced* me to go up a second time and make sure I was wrong. And then, of course, they were actually fighting! If *only* that husband of hers had taken my warnings seriously."

This had been one of the keynotes of Isobel's newspaper interview. Clearly she was ignoring any suggestions that Cordelia was in the clear, if only because that diminished her own role earlier in the evening. Meredith, for his part, was not greatly interested in the row any longer. He was more concerned with what happened later. He said:

"You didn't go upstairs again later on? After that second time?"

"Oh, no." Her hand fluttered to her breast. "I felt . . . well, snubbed, if you want the truth. By her husband. Though now I feel rather proud that I did what I did, however useless it turned out to be."

"I believe you introduced yourself to Dame Myra earlier in the evening, is that right?"

"Yes. There is a connection, you see."

"You'd never met her before?"

"No—of course, *never*. In the circumstances." Isobel seemed to be trying to give the impression that, with her wide acquaintanceship with the great and famous, a meeting with Myra would otherwise have been inevitable.

"The circumstances being the fact that your father had had an affair with her!"

"Well, obviously. No secret about that—Myra saw to it that there never could be. Spread it over the sort of paper the servants read. I would hardly have wanted to meet her."

"Yet on Monday night you went up and introduced yourself."

"Oh, well—*now*. After so many years. And with Father practically a vegetable." She screwed up her face into an unattractive *moue*. "Really, it's a pity in his case there's no life-support system to be switched off!"

"You were not close to your father?"

Isobel bridled. "Oh, I don't know about that. But Father was never what I'd call a *family* man. Being an only child himself, I don't think he really appreciated what a close family could *be*. I was as close to him as any daughter was likely to be, granted that we saw so little of him."

"You never tried to be closer—never lived with him for any length of time?"

"Oh, *no*. I wouldn't have wanted to. I'm not very fond of arty people, you know. And Mumsy and I were very close."

"So you never resented Myra?"

"Oh, *no*! Why should I?"

"Or Cordelia—his other daughter?"

"Heavens no! I was grown up by then." She leaned forward, the greedy, excited look in her eyes. "If she *is* his daughter, of course."

"You question whether she is?"

"Well, nobody can know who their father is, can they? Unless their parents were alone on a desert island at the time. And the things you read about Dame Myra's morals . . ."

She overheard the bit about the Cameron Highlander, thought Meredith. But he was suspicious of Isobel's constant insistence on matters connected with Cordelia.

"You mentioned your mother. Tell me about your family."

"Oh—Mumsy came from solid business people. Her family had a pottery factory in the Midlands—solid, respectable, quite well known. And of course the Cotterels are very distinguished. You can trace the family back to the Second Zulu War."

Meredith looked at her incredulously. Could she be as stupid as she sounded? She gazed back, satisfied she had impressed, quite unconscious of having said anything ridiculous. Suddenly he guessed how it could have happened. Her father, in her childhood, had heard somebody boasting that they could trace their family back to the Crusades or the Wars of the Roses. And he had claimed in jest to be able to trace his back to the Second Zulu War. And Isobel had gone on claiming it, on and off, ever since. She must indeed be a stupid woman—and a decidedly ill educated one, a fact that reflected little credit on her father.

"I meant really your family life at home."

"Oh—well, as I said, there wasn't a great deal of it, not as far as my father was concerned. I believe Mumsy and Father were very happy at first. Father had been married before, for about five minutes, so I think the second time round he did try to make a go of it. But Roderick always says he wasn't naturally mon—mon—"

"Monogamous?"

"Yes. So that by the time I was growing up, there wasn't much family life involving Father at all."

"There were just you two children?"

"That's all. Mumsy brought us up. She was very brave, and she made a beautiful job of it. She'd become a Catholic, so there was no question of divorce."

"And I suppose you both benefit when your father should die?"

"That's right. I get the house, and Roderick and Caroline get all the rights to the books. I must say I don't think that is a fair distribution! I think they *played* on him, using Becky. It would almost serve them right if people lost interest in the books, wouldn't it?"

Meredith left a pause, wondering whether by gesture or word Mrs. Allick would show that she was ashamed of what she had just said. There was no such sign. Meredith sighed, very quietly.

"You mentioned just now that your father had been married twice. Could you tell me about the first marriage?"

"Goodness, no. It was before I was born."

"Yes, I realize that. Did you never hear talk of it?"

"Not much. Roderick would know. They have all the papers up there at the Rectory—and are no doubt planning to get a *great* sum for them when he dies." She wrinkled her forehead. "I believe it was about 1925 or '26—some chorus girl or flapper, or something of that kind. Boy-and-girl romance, or not much more. She went on to marry some lord or duke or other, and they were both killed in the war."

"Ah, she's dead."

"Oh, yes, long ago."

"And no children by your father?"

"Oh, no, certainly not." She looked at him, trying to puzzle something out. "I really don't understand these questions about Father's wives and possible children. It's Myra who was killed, isn't it? And I don't see why you need try to find *more* children, Chief Inspector."

"I'm sorry, I don't get— Oh, I see. You mean there's Cordelia."

"Well, but naturally."

"But I'm afraid that at the time the murder shot was fired, Cordelia Mason was on her way up from the beach."

"Oh, but it's obvious that was some kind of trick, isn't it? I mean, *surely* . . . She must have shot her with a silencer earlier on. Perhaps that later shot *was* a car backfiring. I'm sure a clever man like you will work out how it was done. It's so obvious that it must be her. Everyone knew they were working up to an almighty row, they *had* the almighty row, because I heard it, and heard Cordelia attack her mother. Obviously the row ended with Cordelia shooting her."

"Dame Myra by this time having got into bed and lain there calmly waiting to be shot? No, I don't think so, Mrs. Allick."

But when she had gone, exuding an air of dudgeon and apparently believing that she had handed him the solution to the case on a plate and had it rejected, he did reflect on one thing she had said.

"Everyone knew they were working up to an almighty row . . ."

But that was not in fact true, was it? The Mason group had all no doubt expected something of that sort, but they had put up a reasonably good front for the guests at the Red Lion. The people who could best have counted on the meeting between Myra and Cordelia ending in a row were the people who knew most about the situation between them. And that, surely, meant the Mason party itself. And of course Roderick and Caroline Cotterel.

16

"We've been looking forward to our chat," said Daisy Critchley, as if Chief Inspector Meredith had come to discuss arrangements for the horticultural show. She ushered him and Flood through the hall and threw open the door of the sitting room with an air of saying: "Not everyone gets shown in *here.*"

"Sit you down," said the commodore in his hearty old sea-dog voice, gesturing toward a pink plushy armchair in which one sank as into a fleshy, overintimate embrace.

The Critchleys just remembered to nod at Sergeant Flood, who took an upright chair in which he was a good deal more comfortable than his boss. While the Critchleys fussed around them, offering them drinks that they could not accept and ashtrays that they did not need, the two men had a chance to take in the room. The furniture was all plush and tassel, in lustrous shades, and the room was beset with lampstands and ornaments and Regency stripe. It looked as though the furniture had been bought at an expensive shop at sale time, for the visitor got a subtle sense of none of it cohering, of things having been bought in spite of the colors not being quite right. The room was not large enough to take them all, for the house, on the outskirts of Maudsley, was a dreadful modern parody of Queen Anne, put up by a well-known building chain at the upper end of their design range. Apparently the Critchleys followed the prime minister in their taste for expensive architectural tat.

"Now," said Commodore Critchley as he and his wife sank into the sofa, looking like twin fetuses in a womb that they were going to have great trouble getting out of, "we're at your service, old chap. Where do you want us to start? Night of the murder, or before that?"

"Because we met one of the . . . participants—no, two —before Dame Myra was killed," said Daisy Critchley. "We were actually up at the Cotterels' when Cordelia Mason and her . . . gentleman friend arrived."

She gave the impression that she would be eternally grateful to Roderick and Caroline for, as it were, letting them in on the ground floor of the case. Meredith decided to play them with a loose line.

"What was your impression of the pair?" he asked.

"Sweet little thing," said the commodore. "The girl. Doesn't make the best of herself."

"Hardly *little*," said Daisy. "Distinctly overweight."

"I mean as people," said Meredith.

"Nervous, unsure of herself," said the commodore. "No self-assurance at all. Not what you'd expect in the daughter of an actress. Used to having people round her all the time, or so you'd suppose."

"Neurotic, if you want my impression," said Daisy in her hard, downright fashion. "Fidgeting with her hands the whole time and pulling a handkerchief apart."

"And the young man?"

The commodore screwed up his face and looked at his wife. "Hardly noticed him, tell you the truth. Quiet, dreamy type. Not the sort I'd want any daughter of mine to marry. Not the sort I'd want under my command, come to that. He'll mooch his life away."

"A lot younger than her," contributed Daisy Critchley. "I don't think it ever does, do you? It creates confusion about who's boss."

Meredith suppressed a tiny smile. He suspected there was

no confusion in the Critchley household as to who was the boss. He shifted position in his chair, and the pink monster released one buttock and sucked in another with cannibal relish.

"I see," he said. "I suppose you must have had a little chat with them, when you met them at the Cotterels'?"

"That's right. About her mother, what we'd seen her in, and so on."

"So that when you saw them at the Red Lion, in a party with their mother and her new husband, it seemed natural to go up and introduce yourselves?"

"That's right," said Daisy. "Of course, we'd mentioned to several people that we'd met the great Myra Mason's daughter."

That, Meredith knew, was certainly correct. The Critchleys had talked of that first meeting both in the Red Lion, which was their local, and in other hostelries with a middle-class clientele in a twenty-five-mile radius of Maudsley. Just as, since the murder, they had driven around the same establishments again, giving an account of their involvement in the deed that all the tabloids were shrieking about. It was not boasting exactly, or drinking out on the topic, since presumably they had no need to cadge drinks. Rather it was, or so it seemed, a need to establish their connection with the notable or the notorious, their small but vital place in events that were thrilling the nation. It was a near universal urge, capitalized on by reporters and television interviewers. And the Critchleys were, of course, retired people with time on their hands.

"—so that when we saw them there together, we just had to go over and pay our small tribute."

"I see."

Meredith knew that the imminent arrival of Dame Myra had been well advertised in advance in Red Lion circles. He had no doubt that the Critchley presence there during her stay was no accident.

"And was she gracious?"

"Oh, perfectly," said the commodore expansively. "We

felt a little bit pushy, of course, but actors are used to fans, aren't they? Fans are their *raison d'être,* in a way."

"I just wondered, because Dame Myra had been known to be difficult."

The commodore shook his head airily. "Not with us, I assure you."

"Then you had dinner at the Red Lion?"

"That's right."

"Do you dine there often?"

"Actually it was the first time," said Daisy, outfacing Meredith's obvious implication. "But we'd been promising ourselves a meal there for ages."

"And was your table near the Myra Mason table?"

"No," said Daisy, managing to keep the regret out of her voice.

Meredith shifted position in his chair again and wondered if next time he would go down for the last time.

"Now," he said, "when the Myra Mason party finished their dinner—"

"We'd already had ours," said Daisy rather quickly. "Had less to talk about, I suppose, and the service was first-rate. We were already back in the bar when Granville Ashe came in with Pat. They came to sit next to us."

There was a tiny emphasis on the pronouns. Daisy knew they were being accused of tuft hunting.

"I see. And you all got talking?"

"That's right," said the commodore. "Though the boy— Pat—didn't say much. But Ashe himself was very friendly, even affable, wasn't he, dear?"

"Awfully nice. Something of a raconteur, and quite the gentleman, too," confirmed Daisy.

"Had some damned good stories to tell. Don't know a lot about the theater, but I like to hear a good backstage yarn. He'd been all over, this Ashe feller, from the West End to Pitlochry, from local reps to TV series, so he had a real fund of stories. Thoroughly enjoyed talking to him."

"And quite a little crowd gathered, I believe?"

"That's right. Everyone enjoys a greenroom gossip, a peep

behind the scenes. And I think the word got around that something was happening upstairs after that damnfool sister of Cotterel's came up and blabbed her story."

"Ah—you'd met her before?"

"Briefly," said Daisy. "In the Red Lion, in fact, on one of her earlier visits." Her lips tightened, if that was possible. "We were not impressed."

"Anyway, that added spice to the situation," resumed Commodore Critchley. "So that by the end there was quite a little group around us."

"Pat McLaughlin having by this time gone?"

The commodore thought—the responsible captain of men, making sure he got his facts right.

"Let me see. He went soon after the sister came down with her story. I know, because he wasn't there when I bought the next round of beer."

"You bought the next round. I see. And were there any more rounds? Did Granville Ashe buy the round after that?"

The Critchleys looked at each other with that perfect understanding born of the long bondage of married life.

"We knew you'd ask that. Naturally we talked it over. I bought the next round *and* the round after that. Ashe offered, but I insisted. He was entertaining us, after all. I think everyone who was round our table will back us up: Granville Ashe never left his seat, not even to go to the loo."

"You went to the lavatories yourself?"

"*I* went there, but Daisy was still at the table." He looked at his lady wife, and she nodded agreement. "He never left his seat—not until he went up to find the body."

"Right!" said Meredith briskly. "That's quite clear. I should say that I or one of my men have taken statements from other people in the bar, virtually everyone who was there, and they pretty well all bear out what you've just said. Now, let's get to the sound of the shot."

"As we now know it was," said Daisy. "At the time we all assumed it was a car."

"Quite. But whatever it was, you must all have jumped

and looked around you when it happened," said Meredith. They both nodded. "Did you notice anyone missing from the bar who had been there previously?"

They both thought and shook their heads.

"No," said Commodore Critchley finally. "I can't pretend to notice what I didn't. There was this little crowd around the table. I doubt if we could have seen through it to the rest of the bar."

"So what happened? You decided it must be a car backfiring and went back to theatrical reminiscences?"

"For a minute or two. But then this woman came in, as I'm sure you know, and was very insistent that it was a shot." The commodore coughed. "Don't need to go into how she knew. Embarrassing for the poor woman. Anyway, finally Ashe was convinced—or convinced he ought to go up and investigate, though I think he still thought she'd got a bee in her bonnet. He went to the door, we followed, and so did most of the others in the bar."

"I know it sounds pretty bad form, Chief Inspector," said Daisy, giving a charmless smile, "but by then a real tension had grown up about what was happening upstairs."

"So pretty much the whole bar was collecting around that door?"

"Well, yes, I'd say it was," said Critchley.

"And the door was open?"

"Yes." The commodore made a rather shamefaced admission. "Matter of fact, I think I held it open myself."

Meredith struggled to his feet from the suctioning embrace of the plush armchair.

"Could we reenact it, at your sitting-room door here?" he asked. They went over, Flood standing a little aside, as if he knew his place in that household. Meredith took command. "Granville Ashe goes through the door into the hotel section, and you are all on this side, still in the bar. Would you be Ashe, Commodore? Walk upstairs and show us approximately what occurred, timing it as near as you can estimate to the timings on the night of the murder."

"I'll try," said the commodore, looking self-conscious.

"Of course no one was using a stopwatch." He walked through the door, shoulders squared, and up the stairs. At the top he paused, opened a door, and shouted, "Door!" The second hand on Meredith's watch ticked around ten, twelve seconds, and then the commodore was heard to run cumbersomely downstairs.

"Call the police!" he shouted in the manner of all bad amateur actors.

They all stood around the door somewhat awkwardly.

"That was about it, Inspector," said Critchley.

"There was a faint click when he switched the light on," said Daisy. "But there was no shot. And surely he couldn't have used a silencer?"

"No, there's no question of a silencer," said Meredith. "All I'm doing is checking every little thing to see that all the accounts tally with each other. Now, can you remember who was around the door listening?"

Again they looked at each other, rather as if the commodore were asking permission to speak first.

"The landlord. The woman who'd insisted it was a shot. Hartley, the greengrocer. The chap who keeps the post office. Cotterel's sister . . ."

"Ah, she was there."

"Oh, yes. She was very interested."

"Was she in the bar when the shot rang out?"

"We wouldn't know that," said Daisy Critchley. "She wasn't in the group around Granville Ashe, so we couldn't see through it to see who else was sitting in the bar."

"When did you first become conscious of her?"

"Oh, when the woman was trying to force Ashe to go up and investigate," said the Commodore. "We were sitting with our backs to the wall and the window, you see. At some point she joined the group, and I could see her face. She was watching the woman and Granville Ashe almost hungrily. Sort of licking her lips at the prospect of some excitement."

"Ghoul!" said Daisy Critchley. "Some people have no shame, do they?"

17

Chief Inspector Meredith let himself in by the front door
and went straight through to the kitchen. His wife, he knew,
would be out. She had long ago found that being a
policeman's wife and being a teacher did not go together,
and she had given up her full-time job without too many
regrets. But she did value her evening classes, where she
coached adults through to ordinary and advanced-level history exams. With adults one didn't have to lower one's expectations the whole time, she said. Meredith opened the
fridge and took out the plate she had left for him: a crab
salad. Where had she found that excellent dressed crab?

There were voices raised in the living room, but not in
anger. He opened a can of beer, got a knife and fork, and
went through. The children greeted him and then went on
with what they were doing. It was their usual way. A
policeman's family grew to be that bit blasé about whether
he was around or not. If they did not, they regularly suffered
everything from minor disappointment to heartbreak. Meredith could only feel glad—and grateful to his wife—that his
brood had turned out as well as they had. The eldest had left
the nest, and her marriage still left feelings in him that he
ashamedly recognized as something close to resentment.
Three were left: Mark, nineteen, Eleanor, a year younger,

and Cathy, the baby at fifteen. Tonight they were engaged in a game of Trivial Pursuit. Meredith stood for a few minutes, marveling at what they knew and what they did not know, and fetched his briefcase from the hall. A working dinner. How many working meals, he wondered, had he eaten in the course of his police career?

"That's nonsense! Julius Caesar *can't* have been born in 1 B.C.!" he heard Eleanor cry, her voice thick with grievance. "He came to Britain in 55 B.C. He'd have had to have lived backwards!"

Oh, God, the makers have given another wrong answer! he thought. He waited. Let them squabble for a bit, then go off and find a book to look it up in.

"Well, that's what it says here!"

"It can't be right. Mark, didn't Julius Caesar come to Britain in 55 B.C.?"

"I *thought* he did," said Mark slowly. "It couldn't have been 55 A.D., could it? I mean, by that time the Roman Empire had come to Nero and Caligula and all those people. What's the best place to look it up?"

Meredith breathed out and forked in some delicious crab. They had been well trained. A historian's children should always know where to look things up.

A policeman, too. He had looked up Benedict Cotterel in the new *Oxford Companion to English Literature* the night before and had found a generous, short appreciation rather along the lines of his son's account. Today he had sent a constable to the police library to get a photocopy of his *Who's Who* entry, which he now took out from his briefcase and laid before him on the table. As he ate, he skimmed through the relevant details.

COTTEREL, Benedict Arthur, novelist, travel, and miscellaneous writer. *b.* 9 February 1901, only child of Frederick Arthur Cotterel, tobacconist and newsagent of Romford, and of Mary Esther Cotterel, née Smith. Worked for East Anglian Insurance Co., and for the *Daily*

Herald, until the publication of his first novel, *The Scent of Roses,* in 1927.

There followed a list of his novels and other major writings, two honorary degrees from a British and an American university, and one literary prize (not one Meredith had heard of, but then Cotterel wrote novels before the Booker or the Trask were thought of). He belonged to no club and had apparently never accepted any honors from the state—or perhaps had never been offered any. The absence of writers from the various Honours Lists is one of the few signs that writers are still viewed, by politicians at least, as dangerous, unmalleable people.

The marriages were there, early on in the entry: *"m.* 1st 1924, Florence Urquhard, divorced 1926; 2nd 1934, Patricia Ellen Haynes (1915-1968); one s. one d."

The entry concluded in traditional fashion: "Interests: architecture, walking in remote places, Italian history. Address: The Old Rectory, Maudsley, Sussex."

And that was it. Nothing much there of interest. Except, of course, that "only child". . . .

He finished off his salad. His children had discovered that Julius Caesar had been born around 100 B.C., not 1 B.C., and had gained a healthy glow at having bested the compilers of the Trivial Pursuit questions. Now they were settled back into their game. Meredith took from his briefcase a handwritten list that Cordelia had sent over to him of men with whom her mother had been associated. It was neat, annotated, and very long. Meredith blanched. That would be a matter involving a great deal of legwork. He put it aside and took up the papers that summarized the physical evidence about Myra's death. He scanned them slowly, pondering, hoping that this time the report would tell him more than when he had skimmed through it at the station.

The medical evidence was rather more precise than usual, the police doctor having been on the scene so soon after the killing. Myra was murdered sometime between 9:30 and 10:15, which meant effectively between 9:30 and 9:55, when the body had been discovered. The time of the shot, 9:50, seemed an eminently likely time to the police doctor. Death had been instantaneous.

The Webley and Scott that had fired the shot was not to be found in police records, was probably of service issue, but had certainly been in use more recently than the war. It was well cared for, and there was no question of a silencer having been fitted and then removed.

Meredith had known, regretfully, that a silencer was a red herring. Silencers simply did not figure in domestic killings, and Granville Ashe had not had time to remove such a thing. He was out of it altogether. The shot heard in the bar, almost certainly, was the shot that had killed Myra Mason. And Granville had not fired it. On the other hand, whoever had fired the shot had presumably dropped the gun to avoid incriminating themselves if it was found on them. That would argue that they had stayed in the Red Lion.

It was a pity about Granville, because financially Myra was certainly worth killing. There was the flat in Hampstead, bought in 1964—with the profits, Meredith guessed, of her newspaper revelations. Then the area where it was situated had not been particularly fashionable, being at the Finchley end and thus relatively cheap. No fashion had crept up to it, or desirability, and it had profited by London property values, which had spiraled into madness. Then it had been the modest flat of an aspiring actress. Now it was worth a bomb.

The house in Pelstock was large (five bedrooms, three reception, in addition to a housekeeper's flat). The grounds were extensive, and Myra had acquired three adjacent fields, currently rented out to local farmers but likely to be released soon as building land. She had an extensive holding of stocks and shares, an extremely healthy bank balance, and a large collection of jewelry, both modern and antique. She had about fifteen turn-of-the-century English paintings, bought for a song but currently teetering back into fashion.

Myra had done very nicely for herself.

All of which did bring up the question of Cordelia and Pat.

There was no evidence that Cordelia knew she had been disinherited. She had a cast-iron alibi: She was down on the beach around 9:30, toiling up from it around 9:50. Even if the shot had been a blind, she would be out of it. Pat, on the other hand . . .

Pat McLaughlin had no alibi whatsoever; he had no alibi from the time he slipped out of the bar—say, around ten to nine—to the time Sergeant Flood went down to the tent to fetch night gear for Cordelia—around eleven o'clock or a bit after. He saw nobody, and was seen by nobody. Not surprising in a rural environment, but it left him wide open to suspicion.

He could have murdered Myra as part of a conspiracy with Cordelia, or he could have done it independently, expecting her to inherit. He could even have done it to rid Cordelia of her mother obsession, though this was the kind of speculation Meredith was inclined to dismiss out of hand as fanciful.

Could one accept any of these possibilities psychologically? Meredith considered Pat: remote, uncommunicative, self-sufficient. He did not know Pat, but more: He did not know anything *about* Pat. He had got nothing from him beyond a sense of apartness. The point was, one could not *reject* any of those possibilities psychologically.

And yet . . . And yet, there *was* a lot against them.

First, though it was maybe true that neither of them knew that Cordelia had been disinherited, still given Myra's character, it was a fair guess that she might have been. Would Pat—either independently or in collusion—kill Myra in the *hope* that Cordelia was still her heir? If they were after her money, would they not have made some effort to placate her? In fact, their every move was designed to do the reverse. This was a much stronger argument than Cordelia's refusing a share in Myra's wealth *after* the murder, which could have been prompted by self-interest and a desire to shield herself from suspicion.

Again, if the killing was not financially motivated but emotionally motivated, it stretched belief. Cordelia might kill Myra in the heat of the moment—had indeed committed violence on her. But to *plan* to do it, in cold blood, and then to use somebody else—this did not seem to be in Cordelia's makeup, and Meredith did feel he had learned quite a lot about her in their two sessions together.

Of course, when she left Myra, she could have met up with Pat, maybe on the cliffs; there she could have poured out the story of the quarrel, persuaded him to kill her. Then what? Had Pat gone back to the tent on the Rectory lawn to fetch the gun, run back to the Red Lion? No, it really didn't make sense. Why would they have a gun with them? Any impulse Pat might have to kill Myra would have cooled off long before he got to her bedroom in the Red Lion.

Benedict Cotterel was an only child . . .

Meredith's thoughts swerved violently and came back to the novelist and his family. In particular to the great man himself, senile, powerless, lying on his bed dictating wills and leaving his yacht to a sister who never existed.

Benedict Cotterel was out of it. That was for sure. The Maudsley doctor had attended him throughout the long years of his terrible sickness. He was quite categorical that there was no fraud, no imposture. Cotterel was as sick as he appeared to be, was mentally in a twilight world. But if Ben Cotterel was out of it, there was still his family: his son, his daughter-in-law, and that strange, disturbed daughter.

Isobel Allick was on drugs, he was sure of that. Not heroin, certainly, but something more fashionable and slightly less deadly. He could imagine all sorts of reasons why she should have let herself become hooked: She was bored, underemployed, she had a failed marriage, a repulsive son, all sorts of ambitions and neuroses working away inside her. She had also a resentment—a remarkably long-lasting resentment—against her father. She had tried (though she denied this) to go and live with him in London when she had left school, but he had turned down the idea. Who knew what feelings of rejection this might have aroused? It had not escaped Meredith that this could have been around the time that Benedict Cotterel was having his affair with Myra Mason.

Isobel had been seen—indeed, she had made herself very noticeable—in the group around Granville Ashe when Mrs. Goodison had been trying to persuade him to go upstairs and investigate. But that was some minutes after the shot. No one seemed to have noticed her in the bar at the time when the shot was heard. If she was hyped up with drugs, this might suggest the possibility of an impulse killing, perhaps some mad revenge for a slight. But the gun? If she had brought it with her, this would suggest a very different sort of killing. Unless, of course, she carried it everywhere with her. Did she, Meredith wondered, have some kind of persecution complex in addition to her other problems and oddities?

The fact remained that she was one of the people who could not be vouched for at the time of the shot. But then, so were her brother and sister-in-law, if what was wanted was *independent* witnesses.

The time of the shot . . .

Meredith shook his head violently. He was beginning to go around in circles. What he needed was a cup of coffee. He stuffed his papers back into his briefcase and stood up. The game of Trivial Pursuit was still going on at the other end of the room. His elder daughter was currently agonizing over the largest Spanish-speaking country outside Spain.

"I'll say Mexico," she said at last.

"Wrong! It's Argentina!" said Mark triumphantly.

Meredith came over and put his hands on his youngest daughter's shoulders. His love for Cathy was painfully strong, so strong that he hoped none of the others sensed it or felt slighted. In fact, Cathy herself was the only one in ignorance of it. She sat there, fair, lithe, and with five little triangles in her piece, to the others' four each.

"What are you doing, letting the baby beat you?" he demanded of them.

"It's all *luck*, Dad," explained Mark with a touch of irritation, which probably came from wounded pride. "Some of the questions are dead easy, some are impossible."

He moved his piece on to a pink square.

"TV and Entertainment," announced Cathy. "Right—this one *is* dead easy: 'Who were the stars of TV's *The Good Life*?'"

"Richard Briers and Wendy Craig," said Mark happily.

"Wrong!"

"No, I'm not."

"It's Felicity Kendall. Wendy Craig was in *Butterflies*."

The game went on. But Meredith was no longer following. Because something had clicked in his mind for the second time, and this time it stayed there. His brain whirled. But that was—if that was true . . .

His mind raced over the various possibilities. One thing was certain, though: If this was any sort of revelation, he had been barking up some very wrong trees indeed.

18

The house, now, was not in the best part of Merton. All around it the three-story dwellings had been dissected into flats and bed-sitters, and signs of neglect and decay were not difficult to detect. This one, number 37, had been meticulously restored at some stage to its late-Victorian substantiality. It was solid, four-square, and well-maintained. Behind the wide bay window could be seen heavy brocade curtains, and one did not doubt that behind them the furniture would be good and completely in keeping. Only some slight traces of peeling paintwork suggested that the work of restoration and cherishing was now some time in the past.

Meredith stood inconspicuously on a street corner some way away and considered his best course of action. To go and talk to people in the neighboring houses seemed a bad idea. He might be seen, and in any case they probably held a migratory working population that would not be in at this time of day and would know little if they were. Whether it was true that London people could live for decades side by side with neighbors without exchanging a single word, Meredith did not know. He did know that bed-sitterland in any town was lousy as far as extracting information was concerned: young people, uprooted people, too concerned with

heir own lives and problems to take any interest in other
people's.

There was a sandwich bar, a kebab takeaway, and a laun-
derette, all within easy reach of number 37. They were all
possibles. On the whole, though, the best bet was the pub. It
was one mitigating factor of a policeman's lot that the best
bet for information so often was the pub. Even in soulless,
comfortless London, people were inclined to chat in their
local.

It was eleven o'clock—an ideal, quiet time. The pub was
called the Hare and Hounds— some reminder of days when
red-coated gentlemen and ladies tallyhoed across the green
fields of Merton, or more probably an unconsciously sick
joke on the part of its Victorian builders and proprietors. At
any rate there's no music, Meredith thought as he pushed
his way through the door into its brassy and mirrored interior.

"Lovely day," he said as the landlord fetched him his
pint. "Everywhere looks better in the sun, doesn't it?"

"That's right," said the landlord, putting aside his copy of
the *Telegraph*. He was a fat, comfortable man with a sharp
eye that promised well. "You new around here? The population's that shifting that you never quite know who you've
seen before and who you haven't."

"Not exactly round here," said Meredith casually, sipping
at his beer as he launched into untruth. "Just bought a new
house out Wandsworth way. Old house, rather. In the nature of a speculation. Come to see a chap about restoring it
in period style—aiming it at the yuppie market."

"Oh, yes?"

"Chap who did some work for me a few years ago. So
many cowboys in that business I thought I'd look him up
again. Doesn't seem to be around at the moment. Name of
Goodison."

The landlord looked at him and shook his head slowly.
"Oh, dear. You are out of luck."

"On holiday?"

"Dead. Dead these eighteen months or two years past."

"Well!" said Meredith, calling on all his native Welsh powers of acting and setting down his pint. "I *am* shocked. I had no idea. What did he die of?"

"Heart. Coming on for some time, but he wasn't the type to take care. 'Course, he wasn't a young man."

"That's true. Come to think of it, I should have realized he mightn't still be around. I remember he was quite a bit older than his wife."

"Ten years or more, I'd say."

"Charming woman. What I'd call a real lady."

The landlord laughed. "You wouldn't say that if you heard her in here sometimes. Talk about swear like a trooper —I've never heard a woman to beat her."

Meredith's whole body breathed a great sigh. He had been on the right lines. It had all been a meticulously managed stage show! A wonderful, glowing feeling of euphoria flowed through him; it was a moment of revelation, or triumph. He felt like an angler who has landed an enormous fish, a footballer who has scored the perfect goal.

"Must have been on her best behavior when I met her," he said when he'd caught his breath.

"Could be. Being an actress . . ."

The landlord left the sentence there. Anything, apparently, could be expected of an actress. Meredith registered another hunch that had been proved correct.

"That's right," he said. "I'd forgotten she was an actress. Can't say I've ever seen her in anything."

"Oh, she's on the box now and then. Selena Maddison, that's the name she goes under. Of course in here we get to know all about it when she's going to be on, this being very much her local. She makes sure we watch, and it *does* give you a special feeling, knowing the actress. . . . Not that she's been on that much recently. She had a bit part in the wartime series five or six years ago: *The Oaken Heart.* Lady-like sort of part. That's the sort of thing they've tended to ask her to do: your traditional English gentlewoman. Oh well, if Michael Caine can play a university professor . . ."

"Not like that?"

"Not like that at all. Bit of a hell-raiser, bit of a fire-eating type, if the truth be known. Some of my regulars are a bit wary of her, I can tell you. Mind you, you may not have realized it, but the husband was much the same. They've had some ding-dong shouting matches in here, I can tell you. Basically they were the same type: daredevil, living life to the full."

"Naturally that wasn't the side he showed me," said Meredith. "But I seem to remember he'd had a good war."

"That's right, Commando training, undercover agent in France—that kind of thing. Never really reconciled himself to civvy life. Liked the whiff of danger. Even the business side of him. Always buying properties that everyone else had written off and then trying to get them back into shape. He won some and lost some, so I've heard."

"A good shot, I seem to remember."

"That's it—rifles, pistols, you name it. Take a pot at anything that moved, would Charles Goodison. If someone offered him a go at grouse or deer or whatever, he'd down tools and take him up on it. Take the wife with 'im, as well, as often as not. She couldn't down tools so easily, being an actress, but she wasn't always in work, not by a long chalk."

"Dicey profession," said Meredith.

"That's it. I get the impression she doesn't find it so easy, now he's gone. She's not in here so much—occasional visitor rather than a regular, if you see what I mean—and when she's in, she nurses her tipple. I know the signs. I'm sorry for the lady. Probably gets her booze from the supermarket, going for the special offers. It's a bit of a comedown, because they were always free spenders."

"That's the thing about these independent women," said Meredith, thinking this was a topic on which the *Telegraph*-reading landlord would probably have highly traditional views. "When it comes to the nitty-gritty, they're as dependent on a man as anybody else."

"That's right."

"No sign of a new husband in the offing?"

The landlord laughed. "She won't be without a man for

long, not our Pamela, that's the general opinion in here. Some of the things she used to get up to while he was away you wouldn't credit. Mind you, she's quieter now she's getting on a bit. As to husbands, I don't know. It's always more difficult for a woman, isn't it? At least it is once they get past the forty mark. Not that she isn't an attractive woman still, mind."

"Very much so, when I saw her."

"That's not to say she can pull in a husband, though, is it? She had a younger chap hanging around for a while not so long ago. Fair-haired, slightly poncey type, actorish."

"Probably was an actor."

"Oh, he was. One of our regulars had seen him in something down Guildford way—something Shakespearean, I think he said. Perfectly nice bloke, but you felt if you blew too hard he'd disappear. We thought they might get together permanently—it happens these days once in a while, doesn't it? Younger blokes and older women. But I haven't seen him around lately, so I expect he took fright. That's the problem with these very positive women, isn't it? They put men off, because they always take the lead. Men don't go for that sort of thing."

Some men do, thought Meredith.

"Yes, sir, what can I get you?"

As the landlord bustled away to serve another customer, Meredith hugged himself on his discoveries. It has all been a performance! Those archetypally middle-class clothes, the string of pearls, the travel luggage and the reading matter—all a meticulously built up piece of role-playing. Helped, no doubt, by the roles she had herself played on stage and television in her time. He realized now that his uneasiness about the shot—his toying with the idea that it was some kind of blind to conceal the real time of the murder—was really a subconscious sense of the staginess of it all: the fact of Mrs. Goodison's having been immediately below the bedroom when the shot was fired, the scene—what other word was there?—of her publicly persuading Ashe to go and investigate, the discovery of the murder: pure Agatha Christie first-act curtain.

And above all, the too perfect assumption of the role of the country gentlewoman. The person who never, in any respect, clashes with expectation, always conforms to type, is not a person at all but a performance.

The question was, what to do now? Not talk to Pamela Goodison, that was for sure. She was going to prove a very tough nut to crack. That was clear from the landlord's description of her. Guildford seemed to be a place ripe for investigation. Someone at the theater would surely know about Ashe's affairs. Possibly whatever there was between them had started when she was acting there. He had a comfortable sense that Ashe was certainly not going to prove as tough a nut as his mistress—a very soft nut indeed, probably. But what he wanted was to have the affair well documented before he confronted Mrs. Goodison with the fact that he had penetrated behind her facade.

"So you'll have to find another man to supervise your renovation," said the landlord, coming back.

"That's right, I will."

"Clever bloke, but none too stable, I always thought. Same goes for his wife."

"Don't think I'll go over and offer condolences," said Meredith, finishing his pint. "It'd seem funny, two years after the event."

"Would rather. Fancy your thinking her the quiet, genteel type! She really had you fooled!"

But Meredith was impressed, some days later, when he knocked on the door of number 37, after extensive investigations at Guildford and elsewhere on the theatrical circuit, to find the door opened to him by an impeccably genteel Pamela Goodison. Sensible skirt and blouse, delicate, understated makeup, tactfully permed hair. This was caution! This was foresight! She had anticipated the possibility of further police interest in her. The performance was beautifully maintained during the tea and biscuits she served him in the sitting room and throughout the long and grueling inquisition he subjected her to afterward. Even when he drove her in the police car down to Cottingham, she remained her cool self: well-bred, ineradicably genteel.

It was much, much later, after many hours of questioning, that she screamed at him in a series of short, hard epithets that are seldom heard on polite lips in the Home Counties.

19

When Meredith called at the Old Rectory two days after his second meeting with Pamela Goodison, he said: "I thought I ought to fill you in a little, clear a few things up."

Caroline nodded nervously, called Roderick, and they all went into the sitting room.

"Is Miss Mason around?" Meredith asked. "She's really the most closely involved of all."

Pat had gone off earlier for an evening swim, but Cordelia could be seen down by the tent, reading in the fading light. She had been avoiding the Cotterels recently and had done no further research on her book. Roderick went down to fetch her, and Caroline turned on the television for Becky.

"I'd better settle her down in front of it," she said, smiling almost propitiatingly at Meredith. "I suppose this is going to take some time."

It was a summer blockbuster—a version of a steamy Faulkner novel starring actors from American soaps who wanted to take their clothes off in something classy. Caroline wrinkled her nose and switched over to something that Becky would enjoy more.

"That's what gave me the idea," said Meredith, nodding toward the screen as Roderick and Cordelia came into the room. "Last time I came here."

"What do you mean?"

"You must have noticed how people who watch a lot of television spend hours discussing what they've seen the actors in before? You know: 'Was she the one who played Caligula's sister in *I, Claudius,* or was she one of the nurses in *Shroud for a Nightingale*?' "

"That's true," said Caroline. "People are doing it all the time. I suppose we do it ourselves."

"You were doing it when I was here last. The television regulars become kinds of friends, but rather vaguely remembered. You see them in so many series, you mix them up. What struck me, though it hadn't come to the surface, was how many people in the bar that evening had said—either to me or to one of my men—that they thought they'd seen Mrs. Goodison before. Most of them said it in passing and weren't worried about it; maybe she lived not far away or had stayed there before or had passed through."

"So you had to establish that she hadn't?"

"In an offhand way she'd done that herself. She'd said the bar 'had seemed a pleasant place,' as if she had only encountered it the evening of the murder. Eventually the landlord checked his records and found she had never stayed there before. How to account for the feeling in so many disparate people that they'd seen her before? I remembered a colleague who had cheerily greeted a friend in Harrods, and puzzled for twenty minutes over who it could be. Eventually he realized it was one of the stars of *Emmerdale Farm.*"

"You mean there's no clear boundary anymore between real life and screen life?" asked Roderick.

"I don't think there is. And thinking of television, and noting how people argue about what they've seen people in, everything fading into everything else . . ."

"Yes?"

"It's difficult to put it into words, but I wondered whether the people who thought they'd seen her before, and I in a different way, hadn't been reacting to a television performance in a prestige production. To put it bluntly, I began to wonder if I hadn't been too easily fooled, and if Mrs. Goodison was not altogether too perfect a type."

"We none of us met her," said Roderick. "But even if we had, I don't suppose we would have realized that where we'd seen her before had been on television. You expect life and television to be two quite separate things—like having a friend you always see when you go to Manchester and then unexpectedly meeting him in Paris. It disorientates you."

"Let's sit down," whispered Caroline, nodding toward Becky, who was raptly watching a wildlife program. She led them to the other end of the sitting room. They sat around in the little group of chairs, Cordelia clearly feeling rather awkward, the two Cotterels watchful, and hoping it did not show. Only Meredith appeared completely relaxed.

"Myra Mason noticed her, too," Meredith resumed. "Much quicker than me, naturally. Now I can piece together—conjecturally, of course—what happened. She was studying plays sent by her agent, in particular a new Alan Ayckbourn one. It's about a middle-class woman who gradually throws off all inhibitions and restraints and becomes an elderly punk, with disastrous results. It wasn't a part she could draw on much of herself for, particularly the respectable, repressed woman of the early scenes, so she did what you, Miss Mason, told me she normally did in such cases: She started studying someone—her walk, her gestures, her clothes, and so on."

"And the person she picked on," contributed Roderick, "was Mrs. Goodison."

"Yes. The perfect middle-class type. But being what she was, an actress, it wouldn't have taken Myra Mason long to realize that what she was studying was itself an act—not necessarily that of an *actress* but certainly that of someone to whom the role of middle-aged, upper-middle-class gentlewoman did not come naturally. It wouldn't have taken her long to realize that she had in fact seen this woman before. Being the professional that she was, she was more able to pin down where she'd seen her than the people in the Red Lion: She *was* an actress, and she'd seen her on television.

Before long she remembered what in: a series called *The Oaken Heart* and a short play called *The Blush,* based on a short story by Elizabeth Taylor—the novelist Elizabeth Taylor, of course. I think she was very intrigued by this; hence, the noting of the two pieces down on her notepad. If she mentioned her suspicions to Granville, then she must have sealed her fate; she had to be killed as soon as possible."

They all thought for a moment.

"You are quite sure, are you, that Granville was in it to that extent?" asked Caroline.

"What's the alternative?"

"That when Granville was taken from her by Myra, this Mrs. Goodison determined to get him back and get her revenge on Myra Mason at the same time. Then when she appeared at the Red Lion, Granville was horrified, felt bound to conceal the fact that he knew her, but had nothing to do with the actual murder; that was of her conceiving, her execution."

"That would be more consistent with the Granville we know," put in Roderick.

"Ah, but you don't *know* Granville Ashe at all," objected Meredith. "You've met him, which is rather different. I must admit that I did toy with the notion. He seemed so weak and somehow anonymous. And in the last few days, under questioning, he's tried to foist that idea on me, too. But it simply doesn't hold water. If you think about it, the whole setup was designed primarily to give Granville Ashe an alibi. He must have insisted upon that—being the more craven of the two but also the one most obviously open to suspicion. He insisted that for the whole period of time he would be vouched for—and by plenty of people. He never even went to the lavatory, notice."

"Is that significant?" asked Roderick. "Why should he?"

"He was drinking in the bar before dinner, the Mason table at dinner had two bottles of wine, he was drinking beer after dinner, yet he never went for a pee. A good bladder? No doubt—but your average drinker would have gone, would have made himself comfortable. No—the whole scenario was designed to ensure that he had an alibi, a water-tight one."

"But how long had the plan been hatching?" asked Caroline.

"Probably in embryo since Myra began showing interest."

"Meaning the affair with Mrs. Goodison was never really broken off?"

"No, I don't think so."

"And the motive?"

"Oh, money, of course. From the moment Granville saw the London flat and the house in Pelstock, the thought must have been there. What were they, after all? A third-rate actor, used to provincial digs and perpetual shifts to make do, and a woman, used to moderate luxury, who had been left by her husband very much less well off than she had expected. Myra's two residences would fetch, together, any-thing up to half a million, quite apart from cash, shares, jewels, and the rest. So, when it became clear that Myra was interested in Granville as a *husband,* that must have crystal-lized plans no end."

"Why *was* she, I wonder?" mused Caroline. "Interested in him as a husband, I mean."

"She wanted someone to leave her money to," said Cordelia. "I guessed that."

"I think that's right," said Meredith. "You've mentioned her habit of sailing into things without thinking of the conse-quences. I think that's what happened in this case. Her daughter had found a man, had left her to live with him, and she had heard rumors of the book about her. Probably that's what really got her goat—the book. So Cordelia had to be disinherited—but in favor of whom? She suddenly came face-to-face with the realization that she had nobody. Not at all a nice discovery for a woman of her age. Consequently, she clutched at the first straw: a pleasant, undemanding, subservient sort of man."

"As she saw him," observed Roderick.

"As he *is,* I'm sure. On the surface. Unfortunately for her, he must be a whole lot of other things underneath the surface. But I doubt if he was the initiator of the plans for the murder. That, I feel sure, was Pamela Goodison's doing. It has that daredevil quality that people have mentioned in connection with her. It was a brilliant improvisation."

"Based on the quarrel between Myra and Cordelia?" asked Caroline.

"To a degree, yes. They must have been pretty sure from the beginning that something would come up there. Granville had met Cordelia as a child, remember, and had no doubt heard rumors of Myra's treatment of her later. But if it hadn't, something—some row or other—would have come up elsewhere. That was part of Myra Mason's life-style."

"So once the will was made and signed, all he had to do was foment things in the subtlest possible way?"

"That's right. I gather they went down to the local in Pelstock more than Myra had been accustomed to. Natural enough, now there was a husband to consider, and easy enough to get Myra to agree to, once she knew that Pat and Cordelia had left the area. But Granville knew, of course, that that was one place where they were likely to hear of you, Miss Mason. It was all done in the most indirect way—just as, once he was here, he professed himself quite willing to act as peacemaker but implied there had to be a raging row before the peace processes could operate."

"Perfectly reasonable, if you knew Myra," said Roderick.

"Yes, and if you knew the long-standing nature of her daughter's grievances. But in fact he had got the message through to Pamela Goodison—of where they'd be and when, and of the likelihood of a blowup."

"I feel a bit like a pawn," said Cordelia.

"In fact, you were the most important piece," said Meredith. "Though in the event you turned out to be next to useless."

"After that, I presume, he left all the planning to Mrs. Goodison," said Caroline.

"The real decisions, yes. Once Myra's plans for the evening were known, he communicated them to her. She told him to stick to the bar, have plenty of witnesses—that's why he went to sit next to the Critchleys, known toadies—wait for her to give the sign, and to stay put when he heard the shot. And she told him to make sure that when he went to Myra's room, he was to spend a minimum of time there. All of which he did, because that gave him the alibi he had insisted upon from the outset."

"It was a good plan," said Caroline, "a clever plan. If Cordelia hadn't been put in the clear, it would have worked."

"To a degree," said Meredith. "I don't see that we could have got much of a case together for the courts, but in any event, Miss Mason would be the chief suspect and would remain under suspicion for the rest of her life. That was the only thing that went wrong. Otherwise, the thing went perfectly: She reconnoitered the ladies' lavatories to provide circumstantial backup for her story, and at what she judged to be the best moment, she simply left the bar as if to go to the lavatory and went up and shot her."

"How did she get in?" asked Roderick.

"The door was not locked, but earlier she had borrowed Granville's key, so there was no problem. When she switched on the light, Myra struggled up in the bed, unable to think *why* this woman, whom she'd been watching, should be in her room. Then Mrs. Goodison shot her. She dropped the gun and went coolly off down the main stairs, though she later mentioned the fire escape to throw us off the scent. The finding of the body went like a dream—or like a well-crafted mystery play—and the whole bar came to the door to provide witnesses for Granville's story."

"Do you think they were seriously rattled by Cordelia's being seen on the beach?"

"Concerned, anyway. I don't think Pamela Goodison rattles easily. But there was Granville Ashe's attempt to make Cordelia accept part of her mother's fortune—an offer, I suspect, that would have turned out to be considerably less generous than it seemed at first sight had she accepted. They still had Pat and collusion between the two as a possibility to suggest. But collusion was a notion that they did not want to draw attention to. So they started nudging me in the direction of your sister, sir."

"Isobel? Poor old Isobel? Whatever reason could she have for killing Myra?"

"That was the question. One I gave some thought to—thanks to them. Mrs. Goodison had been handed her on a plate by Isobel's sitting next to her on the night of the murder and confiding in her her connection with the Mason family. So Mrs. Goodison played that card even on our first conversation—realizing that she might need someone to fall back upon. By the time I came to talk to Ashe, he was playing it more openly."

Meredith looked seriously at Roderick. "Do you realize your sister's on drugs, sir?"

"On drugs? Good Lord! No, I never suspected—though I suppose it would explain some things."

"I don't know how long she's been on them or how deeply she is into them, but certainly she needs help, sir. What about her immediate family?"

"She won't get help from them."

"Do they have money?"

"Oh, yes."

"That would be a start. She needs to be got into a clinic. But my immediate point is that that made her at least a conceivable suspect: some imagined wrong from the past, muddled by a brain not fully in control into a monstrous grievance. No doubt if that failed, some further trail could be laid. Maybe against you or your wife, sir—or even against your father . . ."

"I assure you, Inspector, that you wouldn't have got far with *that*."

"No . . . Anyway, as luck would have it, I heard my kids having one of those 'who was in what?' arguments about television programs, and suddenly things began to click into place. Now we've got it all laid out like a map. It was a simple, old-fashioned murder for gain. They were going to live in Spain, you know, once the publicity had died down and the money came through. Whether they would

have lived happily ever after, though, is another matter. I
suspect he would have found that he was going from one
tartar to another. But—who knows?—maybe that was what
he wanted. He apparently had had a series of affairs with
women of much stronger personality than his own."

"How do you know all this, Inspector?" asked Caroline.

"Oh, he broke. That was inevitable. He was the weak link
in her chain all along. Even if he hadn't, we'd have made a
case against them: her deceptions, evidence of their relationship. But as it is, the whole thing's watertight."

Meredith stood up and gave a quick, awkward nod to all
three of them.

"Well, that's it. I thought you were owed some explana-
tion—Miss Mason because she is the nearest relative, and
. . . well, to tell you the truth, Mr. and Mrs. Cotterel, I felt
a bit guilty about entertaining those absurd suspicions about
the distinguished old gentleman upstairs."

If there was a stiffening of the people around him, Meredith did not notice.

"It *was* rather an imaginative idea," said Caroline, walking to the door. "More like a Gothic novel than real life."

"Yes," agreed Cordelia with a nervous laugh. "Rather like
Mrs. Rochester roaming about the house at night and setting fire to things."

"I'll tell you what confused me," said Meredith, stopping
at the door. He had a vague feeling that they were trying to
get rid of him, but he was probably mistaken, and he did
want to clear this niggling little uncertainty up. "When you
took me up to see the old gentleman, I heard him making his
will, as he thinks, and I heard him leave something or other
to his sister. Then I learned that Benedict Cotterel was an
only child. That's what struck me as funny—as hard to understand."

Roderick knew how Caroline, even as she lived a lie, and
had for years, hated actually to utter one. He weighed in
quickly with the lie he had prepared.

"You forget my father is a writer, Inspector. He doesn't
only have his own past, he has the past of the characters he

has lived with, lived *in*. It's a bit pathetic, really, almost grotesque, but sometimes, even now, he becomes characters from his own books—leaves things to other characters in those books."

"Well!" marveled Meredith, smiling in relief at a niggling worry clarified. "That explains it! That's something I never would have thought of."

"It's not unlike Myra," contributed Cordelia in a rather unsure voice. "She sometimes *became* the character she was preparing to act. I welcomed it as a rule; they were often pleasanter than her real self."

Meredith had got to the front door and went happily through it, taking out his car keys.

"I feel like a real bumpkin not to have thought of that. Especially as I've investigated the death of a writer before. That was a crime writer, though. Perhaps they don't go so deep. Well, thank you for all your help. You'll be glad to be seeing the last of me, I imagine. But I'm used to folk feeling that."

He raised his hand cheerily in farewell and drove his car down the gravel lane toward the gate. He could not have felt the long, released breath as he drove away.

"Well," said Cordelia awkwardly, "I'll be going to meet Pat—"

"No!" said Caroline. "We can't simply leave it there, and I don't believe you want to."

"You're wrong. I do want to. It's really not important to me anymore," said Cordelia, an edge of panic coming into her voice. "I don't want to quarrel with you. I don't want a scene—I've had enough scenes to last a lifetime. I know that's not my father upstairs. That's all that matters."

"Did it never occur to you to wonder who the old man up there was?"

"Not really. I just knew it wasn't Ben."

Caroline led her back into the living room, and Roderick shut the door. Cordelia remained standing, still reluctant, and pulling nervily at her handkerchief, as she had done when they had first met.

"I don't want a scene, either," said Caroline quietly. "There's no reason why there should be one. I just want you to understand what happened, how it came about. How did you find out? Did you listen to the tapes?"

"No," said Cordelia bluntly. "It was his feet."

"His *feet*?"

"I went up one day, very quietly, to have another look at my father. You were out on a drive with Becky. He was asleep, but his bedclothes were all disarranged. I went to tuck him in, and I saw he had large feet. The day before I'd read an interview with him, stored downstairs, which had described him as a 'spry little mannikin' with elegant size-six shoes. The man upstairs was not large, but his feet were certainly size nine or ten. Feet don't grow with old age."

"No," said Roderick. "Things shrink, but nothing grows."

"I slipped off the tape and took it down to the tape recorder in the study. It was very pathetic. I didn't recognize any of the things he was leaving—not from this house, not from what I'd read of his life. Ben never owned a yacht. It just wasn't his sort of thing—was it?"

"Not at all," said Roderick.

"And the names of the people he was leaving things to—I didn't recognize any of them."

"You might have recognized one," said Caroline quietly. "My maiden name was Quantick."

"Oh—"

Cordelia put her hand to her mouth in sudden understanding.

"Not that he leaves anything to us. He feels, poor lamb, some sort of vague resentment, as if we were responsible for the way he is now. So he leaves things to old friends, family —most of them people long since dead."

"Then he's—is he *your* father?"

"Yes. Rupert Quantick, my father . . . It's a difficult story to tell, to make clear how we fell into this . . . deception. And of course we have *never* told it before. My father wasn't at all like us—or, for that matter, like Ben. He was a businessman, entrepreneur—very much a man of the world: hearty, gregarious, loving all the good things of life."

"Too much so," said Roderick.

"Yes. He was also, I'm afraid, not very honest. He loved making money, and he wasn't too scrupulous about how he came by it."

"In fact, I think he liked a dishonest buck better than an honest one," put in Roderick. "There are people like that. There is more zest to the dishonest buck, more spice."

"He lived his life, he always said, on the windy side of the law," resumed Caroline. "He loved dodges, slightly crooked wheezes, little fiddles that beat the tax man. They led on, inevitably, to bigger things. Then suddenly the law caught up with him. It was one summer, ten years ago, when we were visiting him in the South of France. He had a villa there, in a little village near Cimènes, and his yacht was moored in the harbor. Maybe it was his life-style that gave him away. Anyway, we could see he was worried. He kept phoning back to England; he couldn't concentrate, didn't want to go sailing or to play golf or any of the things he usually enjoyed."

"We guessed quite soon that what was worrying him was the police," said Roderick. "We'd always feared they'd catch up with him in the end. It was difficult to say what worried us most: the prospect of his going to jail or his inability to concentrate. In the midst of all his worries he would suddenly seem to lose track of things entirely. We even once found him sobbing—an inconceivable thing. He was bewildered by what was happening to him. Anyway, he was so unlike his usual hearty, outgoing self that we were worried, especially as it seemed to get worse rather than better. And then suddenly we realized what it was: the onset of senility."

"Ben was coming to stay for a couple of days. He'd been walking in the Dolomites—a region he'd always loved and which he'd just written a book about. We were looking forward to it, because we didn't see him often. He'd just bought this house, to be near us, he said. But Ben was congenitally restless, and we didn't believe he'd use it much."

"He came," said Roderick, "and he seemed in excellent form. Probably he'd overstrained himself in his walking, but if so, it certainly didn't show. In fact, his spryness showed up the change in Caroline's father. Sometimes Rupert seemed aware of his predicament. We had a splendid meal, and he kept saying, 'Eat, drink, and be merry . . .' We didn't know how to respond, because we didn't know if he was thinking about a possible jail sentence or his own failing powers. Most of the time he rambled and became pathetic, and finally we put him to bed with a couple of sleeping pills."

"Later, just as we were putting out the light, we heard a cry. It was from Ben's room. He'd had a heart attack, a severe one. I got him to bed while Roderick rang the doctor in Cimènes. He was very quick, but not quick enough. Ben died as he came into the room."

"It was devastating—totally unexpected, and coming on top of everything else . . ."

"Otherwise, Roderick would have realized," insisted Caroline. "The doctor said one or two odd things: *'Votre père est bien respecté à Cimènes'*—things like that. Roderick thought he was just being a little flowery—and in fact Ben *was* well thought of as a writer in France. Then, as he was leaving the house, promising to send up the death certificate for us to fill in the personal details, he said: *'C'était un bon garçon, Monsieur Quantick.'* Roderick didn't twig immediately . . ."

"It was the way he said it: Contick."

"—and by the time he did twig, the doctor had got into his car and driven away."

"Then we realized: Caroline's father had been on his books, but he had never actually been to see him. The doctor was young and had recently taken over the practice. He knew of Rupert Quantick, the rich Englishman, and where he lived, but he'd never met him. When the certificate came up next day, it certified the death of Rupert Quantick."

"It was one of those times—a time of decision. Becky was somehow upset by the death, some sense she has of disaster; Father woke up rambling worse than ever, and then someone rang up from my father's firm in Birmingham to say he'd heard the Fraud Squad would be flying out to Nice before the end of the week and would be coming to Cimènes to interview him."

"It seemed like pure impulse at the time," said Roderick. "I said: 'They'll be wasting their time. Caroline's father died last night.'

"The rest followed like a dream. We filled up the missing entries on the death certificate with Rupert Quantick's details, and we buried Ben as him. There was just us and Becky at the funeral. Then we drove Rupert home to England. There was no problem at all. There were the four of us in the car, one a handicapped child, one a sick old man. The passport official just flicked through Ben's passport, glanced into the car—one old man is very like another—and that was that."

"It's funny, isn't it?" said Caroline. "Babies and old people are very much alike."

"So we brought him here, and without realizing it, he began his life as Benedict Cotterel," said Roderick. "We knew, of course, that he wouldn't be able to cope on his own. We moved in and sold our cottage. At first he could go out sometimes into the garden, play a little with Becky. But before long even that became impossible. We took over the administration of his affairs—Ben's affairs—and he took to his bed and lived permanently in some other, some half-real, world. Then it was safe to have help looking after him."

"His, my father's, little business empire collapsed, and all his assets were seized to pay his debts. His yacht, his early Wedgwood, his silver, his pictures . . ."

"The Gainsborough that turned out not to be a Gainsborough at all," put in Roderick wryly.

"So typical of Dad. I was glad that I didn't profit at all by his 'death.' There's a sort of ironic humor, I suppose, in hearing him leave all those things to friends and relatives— things that are long gone. When he dies, he will die as Benedict Cotterel, and then this house will come to Isobel, and most of the rest will come to us."

"Wasn't Isobel a problem?" asked Cordelia.

"We thought she would be," said Roderick. "Our hearts were in our mouths the first time she said she was coming. Then we realized she hadn't seen him since the late fifties. And in fact she always refuses to go upstairs and see him. She's just interested in keeping an eye on 'her' property."

"The doctor here was no danger," said Caroline. "Ben had bought the house, but he'd never lived here. The doctor has treated him throughout as Ben Cotterel. He feels rather proud of having such a distinguished patient."

"When he dies, he will be buried as Benedict Cotterel. Big funeral, no doubt—all the great and good in the literary world, representatives of the Arts Council, Margaret Drabble . . ."

"The *old* Rupert Quantick, my father as I knew him as a child, would have thought that a tremendous joke," said Caroline.

"Then Isobel can have this place, we'll find ourselves a smaller house, and life will go on as before."

"You won't reveal the truth, then?"

"We've talked about it. I don't suppose anything very dreadful would happen to us. But I think we'll only do it, if at all, when Becky is dead. There will be an immense fuss, and she responds very badly to any disruption in her routine." Caroline paused. "I've hated living this lie, but somehow it's around our necks now, like the albatross. Maybe it would be best just to leave a statement with our wills."

"I'm sorry I thought you'd done it to prolong the royalties," said Cordelia awkwardly. "Even though I did think it was Becky you were concerned about."

"The royalties will last out *all* our times," said Roderick quietly. "The doctors say Becky can't live much beyond thirty-five. What we fear most is that we should both die first. I'm afraid that would devastate her, however much money there was around to pay for her looking-after."

"There's Pat coming from his swim," said Cordelia hurriedly. Through the window, in the last light, they could see the beanpole figure with the towel over his shoulders. Cordelia hurried to the front door and hailed him, and they stood together, he with his arm around her shoulders, under the outside light, looking oddly fragile, yet indissolubly united.

"We plan to move on the day after tomorrow," said Cordelia.

"We shall miss you," said Caroline truthfully. "You won't be doing any more research?"

"No . . . The book's a washout. . . . You may as well know that I'm pregnant. I realized a few days ago, just before Mother was killed. When I spent the night in the station cells, I kept saying to myself: 'God might do this to *me,* but He wouldn't do it to my baby.' It kept me going. And He didn't! But I think now it's time to forget. I don't want to stain the beginning of a life with all the grievances and misery of my past. Turn around and start again—that's the best plan."

"I think you're very wise."

"Maybe I'll publish the account of Myra's acting career. An unblemished record of artistic success."

"De mortuis nil nisi bonum," said Roderick.

"Yes. Though that saying doesn't make much sense in modern times, does it? It's only *after* their death that you *can* say how rotten they were." She flashed at them her brilliant smile, and Caroline realized that she had hardly seen it since Cordelia had heard the news that her mother was coming to Maudsley. "I'm not going to start sentimentalizing Mother, you see," she went on. "But don't worry, I won't change my mind about the book. Someone, some day, will write the truth about her, but it won't be me. From me there will be nothing but praise, endless applause. Happy ending!"

She and Pat, closely entwined, began their walk down the lawn to their tent. Then she turned and called back to them: "But I don't promise that one day, when I'm much older, I won't want to write about Ben!"

Roderick and Caroline turned off the light and went back into the house.

"That will be *four* people, now, who know," said Roderick.

"Yes. But I don't worry about Pat. I can't think of anyone less likely to volunteer other people's secrets. Apart from the talk about Myra's death, I really don't think I've heard him say more than a couple of hundred words since he came here. Still, he'll be a good father."

"Very good," said Roderick. "Happy ending."

He went into the kitchen to prepare Becky's good-night Ovaltine, and Caroline went into the living room, switched off the television, and began getting her ready for bed.

Upstairs, in the large bedroom that looked out to sea, the old man, unusually, had awakened. Poised unsurely between the vague dreams of his night and the vague dreams of his day, he extricated his old hand from the bedclothes and directed it shakily toward the tape recorder by his bed. When the reassuring whirring sound started, he cleared his throat.

"To my dear sister Dorothy Quantick, I leave my Gainsborough portrait of Sir Samuel . . . of Sir Samuel Etterick . . . To my dear friend William Harrison, I bequeath . . . I bequeath . . ."

The voice faded into nothing, the old man's eyes closed, and he sank once more into sleep.

On the bedside table the machine whirred on.